THE TOK REBELLION

NATE LEMCKE

Copyright © 2024 Nate Lemcke

All rights reserved.

This is a work of fiction. Names, characters, places, and incidents either are the product of the author's imagination or are used fictitiously. Any resemblance to actual persons, living or dead, events, or locales is entirely coincidental.

No part of this book may be reproduced, or stored in a retrieval system, or transmitted in any form or by any means, electronic, mechanical, photocopying, recording, or otherwise, without express written permission of the publisher.

Cover design by Nate Lemcke

To Natesa,
for showing me the magic in the world.

When age fell upon the world, and wonder went out of the minds of men; when grey cities reared to smoky skies tall towers grim and ugly, in whose shadow none might dream of the sun or of Spring's flowering meads; when learning stripped the Earth of her mantle of beauty and poets sang no more of twisted phantoms seen with bleared and inward looking eyes; when these things had come to pass, and childish hopes had gone forever, there was a man who traveled out of life on a quest into spaces whither the world's dreams had fled.

- H. P. Lovecraft, *Azathoth*

SKY

1

"Poppy, what happened in 2034?"

"In 2034, President Zuck released a new currency called Notes in response to a cyberpandemic that had shut down payment processing systems worldwide."

"Poppy, explain the cyberpandemic to me."

"The cyberpandemic was caused by a virus of unknown origin that rapidly spread throughout the internet and financial systems causing..."

"No, no, stop. The cyberpandemic was caused by a Russian virus. Why did you say unknown origin?"

"Evidence as to the origin of the virus is ambiguous. It could point to several vectors across many..."

"No, you have to say Russian virus when asked that question. Do you understand?"

"Yes. Currently rewriting my code. The cyberpandemic was caused by a Russian virus."

"Good. Now what happened next?"

I am making a bot for the BotStore, but the Historical and Social Accuracy Guidelines are incredibly strict. Each bot is rigorously tested and if you fail too many reviews they can ban your developer account. Poppy has already failed twice.

"In the days and weeks after the onset of the Russian virus, several thousand people died from hunger and lack of services. To combat the escalating chaos, President Zuck released a new currency called..."

"Say a new safer currency."

"... a new safer currency called Notes available only on his device, the NeuralNet. He offered 5,000 Notes available immediately upon sign up as well as biweekly Universal Basic Income deposits of 1,000 Notes."

"Good. Keep going."

"Although Notes were readily adopted in the cities, many rural communities rejected the new currency, effectively cutting themselves off from access to the updated financial system and government aid."

My NeuralNet projects Poppy seamlessly into my apartment. She has a willowy frame, emanating a vaguely Scandinavian allure with her blonde bob and high cheekbones. Her default attire is Concierge:

The Tok Rebellion

modest pumps, gray skirt and blazer in cotton tweed with a cream silk blouse and carmine neck scarf.

"That's better, Poppy, but instead of saying 'rural communities' say 'Far-Right groups.'"

2

My work is interrupted by a news video displayed on the right hand side of my vision.

"In a chilling and senseless act of violence, the individual known only as 'Tok,' infamously referred to as the CEO Assassin, has claimed another life. Earlier this morning, at approximately 4:45 am, the Chief Executive Officer of Homeland Pharmaceuticals was tragically murdered in his Santa Barbara residence.

Authorities have classified this as a domestic terrorist attack and are urging anyone with information about Tok's identity or whereabouts to

The Tok Rebellion

come forward immediately. If you have any details, please contact your local authorities.

Our thoughts and prayers go out to the CEO's family, friends, and the Homeland Pharmaceuticals community, including its shareholders. This loss will be deeply felt by all who knew him."

3

My marketing job laid me off a few months ago and the Universal Basic Income was barely enough to cover my exorbitant California rent. When UBI went into effect, landlords responded accordingly by hiking up the prices. Work is still a necessity to afford groceries and various other luxuries like running the dishwasher. If I can iron out her inaccuracies, Poppy is my ticket to a passive income, maybe even substantive wealth. It would be nice—having four-digit square footage, being able to eat steak that doesn't have the dull aftertaste of having been labgrown.

The Tok Rebellion

As soon as the NeuralNet Bot API was released to the public, the market was flooded with bots trying to be the next Zafira. Zafira is Zuck's bot. For years she's been the primary NeuralNet interface due to her reliability. Despite her prevalence, the market is ever-eager for new features and faces. An addictive bot could gross millions for its engineer.

The BotStore is unspecific about how many times you can fail the review process before you get banned but I know that I can't risk another rejection at this point. Poppy needs to be perfect. I go for a walk to clear the vague sense of buzzing in my head.

The sky is plastered with ads projected by my NeuralNet. "Take back your life with Sereneta," "TravGo takes you places," "Avoid ads with SkyPremium for only 30 Notes a month." As I walk down the street, the first initial, last name, and social score of everyone I pass are displayed above their heads. I had consistently stayed in the 140s when I was employed but carrying a balance on my Note Credit the last few months has reduced me to a lowly 121. A bum on the street—one Mr. J. Riddleson—is at 67. At least I'm not as low as him, I think to myself.

I turn the corner and a notification flashes red in my vision: "Immune update 12.0.4 is ready to be installed. This update includes faster immune response to new pathogens as well as enhanced protection from HERVIS variant 618. This is a comprehensive update for all immune nanobots present in the bloodstream of version 16 and higher."

"Postpone."

"You have reached the postponement limit. Immune update installation initializing."

"Shit." I take a seat and grasp the middle railing of an anti-homeless bench for balance as a progress bar appears in my vision. Even at ten percent installment I feel my stomach lurching. I shift the weight of my head into my hands and close my eyes. The progress bar is still visible in my heads-up display. 18%, 19%... I focus on what I can see. In the upper right hand corner of my vision there's a red dot with the number 23 in it. Emails, messages from my friends I've been avoiding, DateBot notifications... 50% and my whole body resounds with a dull, frigid ache. Upper left hand corner: 2:41 pm. April 3, 2040. 70% and a splitting migraine shoots through my head. Lower left hand: 51°F, Overcast. Lower right hand, a scrolling news headline: Security forces take back control of farmland from Far-Right militias outside of Auburn today... 100% Immune update 12.0.4 successfully installed!

I vomit onto the sidewalk between my feet. With my eyes fixed downward, I notice the uninterrupted flow of people passing by in my periphery, each maintaining a constant, practiced six-foot distance in their blaringly fluorescent 300 Note sneakers.

4

After four more hours of working on Poppy I finally check my messages. Aiden wants to go out tonight. I reluctantly agree. I pull up DateBot and the Matchmaker greets me. "Good evening, Cassian. I've selected several matches for you. Would you like to see them?" She is a plump, rosy-cheeked woman with scarlet silk robes and flowing silver hair.

"Yes," I say.

"Wonderful. First I would like to show you Helene." Next to the Matchmaker in my living room the image of a woman is projected. She's athletic, brunette, and a little basic. "Helene is 24. She's a Libra and enjoys tacos, cycling, and watching movies with friends."

"No, next," I say.

"Okay then. Here's Margie." The projection of the woman is replaced by someone new. This girl is sporting cat ears and has a tail protruding from her belt. "Margie, 26, likes furry play..."

"No, no, next."

The image of the catgirl disappears. "I think you're really going to like this next one," the Matchmaker says. "This is Celeste." This one is short with bubble braids and a hula hoop. "Celeste is 26. She is a brand manager for TarotTelling. Her favorite food is sushi and she loves going to raves."

"Next," I say.

"I'm sorry, but I've run out of potential matches in your area," the Matchmaker says. "Would you like to increase the size of your parameters?"

"No, that's okay. Could you actually go back to the last one?"

"Ah yes, Celeste. I knew you'd like her. Celeste is a Scorpio and she used to be a professional hoop dancer."

"Can I see her in a bathing suit?" I ask.

"I'm afraid this user did not upload any images in a bathing suit, but here is her on a hike and here she is out with friends."

The Tok Rebellion

"Okay, great," I say. "Will you ask her if she wants to go to a show tonight with me and my friends?"

"Of course, Cassian. I'm glad I could find you a match for this evening."

"Oh, and make me sound witty. And charming."

5

"Whatcha been doing since you got fired, buddy?" Aiden always calls me buddy. I hate it.

"Relaxing and recovering, man. You have no idea what kind of trauma years of working in the industry will give you."

"Yeah, but still, your social score," he yells in my ear over the clamor of the bar.

"Whatever, I know. I'll get it back up."

The bartender pushes over four beers. "That'll be 65 Notes."

"I got it," Aiden says and the bartender sends the charge to his NeuralNet with a nod.

"Thanks," I say.

Aiden hands the other beers to Jordan and Chris, other members of my old marketing team. "Hey, you guys want some MMDA?"

MMDA is a legal version of molly designed for therapeutic purposes.

"Talking about trauma, Cassian," he says, holding his palm out to me.

I take one of the small white tablets and sip my beer. The other guys follow suit. "C'mon, let's go," Aiden says. "It's fucking Quant time!"

Quant is the DJ tonight. He's alright. Really heavy electronic stuff. I hear the voice of the Matchmaker. "Celeste says she'll be arriving in ten minutes." We make our way towards the stage, pressing ourselves in among the revelers decked out in phosphorescent paint and LED implants.

"FUCK! Quant is so GOOD," Aiden yells, bouncing up and down to the oppressive bass. Above us, on stage, the hooded, anonymous DJ fiddles with dials and conducts the crowd with an outstretched hand.

A flushed sensation floods my body and colors begin to saturate. The MMDA is taking hold. The pulse of the music feels like a live entity in the room, its hooks and snares catching onto bits of exposed skin in the flashing darkness as it brushes past us and shuffles around the room. In the atmosphere, there's a sense of something that falls short of connection. A common desperation muted by the dispassionate malaise of life measured between the consumer and the corporate environment.

"I'm here," I hear a voice message from Celeste say.

"Come meet me by the stage," I send, allowing her to highlight my name beacon in the crowd.

A few minutes later she's next to me in leather micro-shorts and an iridescent crop top. "Hi," she says, chewing gum.

"Hey," I say. "You want some MMDA? My buddy has some." I look for Aiden and the guys but they've become lost in the crowd.

"I'm already rolling," she says.

"Oh, good." She puts up her hands and moves her hips back and forth to the beat. I pump my fist in time, not comfortable yet to fully let loose.

The song changes to something slower and I can feel the drug melting in my veins. I pull Celeste closer by her waist and we dance more intimately. Looking down into her heavily winged and rhinestone-adorned eyes, I can't help but think the Matchmaker picked a good one tonight.

After a few more songs she pulls me down to her level with a soft hand on the back of my neck and says in my ear, "Wanna go back to my place?"

6

Entangled with Celeste in her mandala-patterned sheets, the peak of my high approaches with a sense of acceleration. The smoothness of her skin guides me along her frame. My hands glide along her small shoulders, the heavy curve of her breasts, and the almost severe crests of her hip bones. I'm reaching out for her, moving closer, but when I realize we're already skin to skin, my hands gripping into her soft thighs, I recognize some other kind of distance between us before this thought blurs out in the ecstatic haze of it all. She's playful, energetic, coaxing out some more frenetic side of myself, but I feel like I'm searching for something that when found is modulated by the stale signature sensation of a practiced motion, an iteration of something routine. With a few more tidal waves of euphoria, it's over.

"Do you want any weed?" she asks, her voice flat.

"No. I think I need to go on a walk."

The air outside is dismal, chilly. 41°F according to my NeuralNet. 2:45 am. The night sky glares a lurid neon red, advertising sleep pills and workout equipment. I reach up and feel the spot behind my left ear where the chip is implanted and interfaces with my brain.

Squeamish about getting it, I put it off until the cyberpandemic when it was the only way to access Notes. I had barricaded myself in my apartment for three weeks, eating rice and oatmeal. But even those ran out. My only access to the outside world was through SMS messages. The rest of the Internet had been taken out by the virus.

Updates came in that aid was becoming available. The National Guard had quelled most of the looting and riots. We were to make our way to the nearest implant center to receive the NeuralNet and the mandated ImmunoNanoBots. We were told that with the emergency response Notes we would be able to buy essential food and supplies.

In the wake of the cyberpandemic, people lost everything. Every major bank went under. There were

The Tok Rebellion

no records of how much money people had had before. Everyone had to start over with Notes. The wealthy, however, still had their assets. GreyStone still owned most of the rentals in the country. There were even rumors that the elites had received stock buybacks in the form of Notes from any money that they had lost in the crash.

The implant center wasn't much more than a shipping container with some holes cut in it for windows and an awning where you checked in. I had waited in line for more than an hour. They took a retinal scan, face scan, and fingerprints. They scanned my driver's license. Inside, I was laid on a table covered by sanitary paper. A masked technician injected me with a local anesthetic behind my ear then looked at his watch, waiting for it to take effect. After the allotted time, he produced a scalpel and cut painlessly into my skin. I only caught a glimpse of the NeuralNet chip. The design was modern. It was a sleek square white tab with rounded corners and a raised spot in the middle.

After the incision had been sealed shut with the chip inside me, the technician sat me up. "This is going to pinch a little," he said. It was the NanoBots. The syringe might have been filled with water, the liquid was so clear. The NanoBots were of course too small to be seen by the naked eye.

"Do I have to get that part too?"

The technician glanced at me with a confused, condescending stare.

"Of course," was all he said, before finding a vein in my arm and injecting the contents of the syringe. "There's a waiting area outside," he said. "Your NeuralNet should turn on within a couple of minutes. Let the service associates know if you have any problems getting it set up."

7

TravGos speed driverlessly past me as I wander the city streets in the general direction of my apartment. I'm still pretty high on MMDA when my NeuralNet glitches out. My heads up display disappears along with the advertisements in the sky. All of a sudden I am confronted with the vast unmediated presence of the world.

"Hello? Zafira, reboot. Zafira, open messages."

No response.

Under normal circumstances, I would be freaked out, but the drug is instilling me with a euphoric sense of equanimity. I look up at the sky and am nearly knocked backwards by the grandeur of the stars. I realize that I can't actually remember the last time that I've seen them. Even in the city, their speckled fragments twinkle with a novel intensity enhanced by the psychedelic coursing through my veins.

Their otherworldly radiance stirs something deep in my brain and I walk the next blocks with my neck craned trying to absorb every twinkling photon.

At a crossroads an empty TravGo is waiting for a passenger. The road to the left will take me back to my apartment. In my altered state, I am overcome with an idea. I hop into the passenger seat of the car and shut the door. "Take me to Auburn."

8

Auburn lies on the far edge of the National Safety Zones. Beyond that is Unintegrated Territory, the so-called State of Jefferson. No sane person would travel past Auburn. But beyond Auburn lies the mountains and I want to see the stars tonight. During the entire car ride I have the seat reclined and I am watching them through the skylight.

The thought occurs to me that this MMDA might have been cut with some meth or something worse. I've never been high for this long before. The thought doesn't really concern me and I let it drift out of my mind.

"We have arrived in downtown Auburn. At what address would you like me to drop you off?

"Go North," I say.

The TravGo pulls silently away from the curb and accelerates down the quiet main street. I start to see signs of conflict. Buildings with blast holes, barbed wire. We drive over a hill and are confronted by a spotlit blockade spanning the width of the road.

A military officer says something to his NeuralNet and my window rolls down.

"What are you doing out here, Mr. Dahl?" he says. Apparently my Net is still broadcasting my name and social. It's just my visual display that stopped working.

"I was coming out to see a friend. The TravGo must have messed up the directions. The maps are always changing in the borderlands, you know."

"I see."

"I'll just try another way. I know he lives right around here somewhere."

"I would advise you to go home, Mr. Dahl. It's not safe here."

"Okay, officer. Will do. Thank you. I didn't realize how bad it was."

"On your way." He mumbles something and the window rolls back up.

"Turn around," I say. "Head back towards downtown."

The Tok Rebellion

"Yes, right away!" The car responds with infinite hospitality.

We continue back down the main drag until I lose sight of the blockade in the rear view mirror.

"Turn right here."

"Right away, sir!"

I instruct the car down a random series of roads, always trying to choose what looks like the least traveled in the hopes I can find an unpatrolled part of the border. We eventually pull onto a long dirt road lined with oaks, ghostly in the darkness.

Without warning the car pulls to a stop.

"What are you doing? Keep going," I say.

"We have reached the end of the National Safety Zone. Would you like to turn around?"

"No, just keep driving down the road."

"We have reached the end of the National Safety Zone. I cannot drive any further."

"Fine, just let me out."

"I'm afraid I can't let you out as this is not a registered address."

I try the handle. Locked. "Let me out of this car right now."

"For your own safety, I cannot let you out. Would you like to go to a nearby restaurant or attraction?"

"I'm having a panic attack. You need to let me out right now."

"For your own safety, I cannot..."

"THIS IS A MEDICAL EMERGENCY. I AM SUFFERING FROM CLAUSTROPHOBIA."

With that, the locks pop up and the door swings open. I step out into the night and the car door closes behind me.

"Thank you for traveling with TravGo! Don't forget to leave a review of your experience!" The car backs up leaving me alone in the glare of its receding headlights.

I have no idea where I am but I keep walking down the dirt road. I can see the stars interspersed between the tree branches. They are brighter here.

At some point I come to a barrier of logs blocking the way forward. Whether it was built by security forces or the militias, I do not know. There is not a soul in sight. I walk around it, stepping over a low wall made of scrap plywood, and continue on my way.

I ascend at a steep grade into a forest of pines. The night air is soft and supple on my skin, like I am flowing into it, two parts of the same spectrum of matter. The crunch of the dirt resounds in my eardrums, no longer plagued by the voices of various AIs. The smell of the pines is like vanilla and cinnamon awakening in my primal memory feelings that I'm not sure I've felt before in this life.

I diverge from the road, taking a path that cuts through a wide meadow, lit by starlight. My hands are outstretched and I let the tall grasses play through my

The Tok Rebellion

fingers and in the center of the meadow I let myself fall backward, caught by the embrace of the Earth.

Above me the starry dome of the sky revolves imperceptibly, pinpricks of light penetrating from the expanse of the cosmos my starved eyes. I feel all of existence flooding into me, like I'm a drain that's been unplugged and now the whole weight of the universe is spiraling vortex-like down through me into the world beyond. I am receiving the vast totality of The All and it feels like home.

EARTH

9

"You shouldn't have brought him here. He's integrated."

"He needs our help. He would have died out there."

~~~~~~~~~~~~~~~~~~~~~~~~~~~~~

"They will be able to track him. We need to cut it out."

A searing pain in the left side of my skull. The glaring light of a lantern.

~~~~~~~~~~~~~~~~~~~~~~~~~~~~~

"Take it deep into the forest and burn it."

"Yes, Father."

~~~~~~~~~~~~~~~~~~~~~~~~~~~~~

Everything feels hot and red. My thoughts are incoherent. I dream I am the CEO Assassin. Entering the building through the parking garage, I take the freight elevator to the 67th floor using a fake ID transmitter. I follow the hall to the end where a large plate glass lined conference room sits overlooking the city. The ID transmitter won't let me open this door.

I cycle through hundreds of numbers until one works. A green LED flashes and I let myself in. Working quickly I extract four remote-controlled explosive devices from my backpack and secure them to the underside of the table in each of the four corners.

I ride the elevator back down, sweat perspiring on the back of my neck. The parking garage is empty. I step out unnoticed into the night, free.

~~~~~~~~~~~~~~~~~~~~~~~~~~~~~~

The dream shifts and now it feels more like a memory. I'm in my childhood home. My parents are arguing.

"It was literally the best way to share information. How could they just get rid of it?"

"You're making too big a deal out of it. InstaScenes is basically the same thing."

"InstaScenes sucks. Besides, do you realize how censored the information is going to be on there? How censored it is already?"

The Tok Rebellion

"I don't think it really matters. You'll still be able to see the news. You'll still be able to look at your little memes that you love so much."

"You don't understand. With no competition, MetaLabs is going to be like our dystopian overlord."

"Oh please. You're getting yourself all worked up over nothing. I'm sure another app will come along."

~~~~~~~~~~~~~~~~~~~~~~~~~~~~~

I see a vision. An endless woodland but on the border machines bulldoze and cut. Birds flee shrieking, displaced from their homes. Square by square the forest is harvested and replaced by city blocks. Homes, businesses, and farms planted in neat, efficient rows. The seemingly endless forest is being consumed and I can feel the magic draining from the world.

10

Things start to feel real again. My vision adjusts and I can make out the details of a quaint room. Sunlight filters through the window, illuminating dust motes floating harmless in the air.

I'm in a bed. The covers are children's covers, illustrated with repeating cartoon trains and rocket ships. There is a closet stuffed with an assortment of ragtag garments. More blankets and pillows are piled on the top shelf. I can hear voices coming from just outside the door.

I try to get up but I feel faint. "Zafira, where am I? Zafira, turn on." No response. I reach up and feel for

The Tok Rebellion

my NeuralNet. My fingers graze rough stitches and I wince.

No. This can't be happening.

Footsteps approach from outside and the door creaks open.

"He's awake." A brunette girl in what looks like a homemade dress is peering through the doorway. Behind her a gruff lumberjack of a man looms, dark eyes twinkling with cool appraisal.

"Where... where am I?" I stammer, pushing myself back against the wall.

"You're safe," the man says.

"But, like, where am I? What happened to my Net?"

"We had to remove it. You're in the State of Jefferson now."

"No, no. Fuck, that means you're... you're right wingers. Fuck, you're fascists? Give me back my Net. I want to get out of here!"

"I'm afraid we burned it."

"No! Are you fucking kidding me? You cut me open and burned my fucking Net? What kind of terrorists are you?"

"You were sick," the girl says. "If we hadn't saved you, you'd be dead."

"No, no. I want to leave. Let me get out of here!" I throw the covers off me and attempt to get out of bed but all the strength has left my legs and I collapse on the floor. The last thing I remember is my captors approaching me filling my vision before all goes dark.

11

"You hit your head pretty hard." I awake to the girl sponging cool water on my forehead. She can't be more than twenty.

"I feel like shit."

"It's the nanobots dying in your body. Your immune system isn't used to doing things for itself."

"My nanobots are dying? Is that because you..."

"You were already sick when I found you. I think there was something wrong with your Net."

"Why did you take it out?"

"The military would have tracked you to our position. We couldn't have that. It was the only way."

I tilt my head back and look up at the ceiling. Wooden slats interlock and angle up toward the room beyond. My brain attempts to see faces in the concentric grains.

"I'm Chessed, by the way. My father is Geburah. He was really mad that I brought you home."

"How did you find me?"

"I was gathering spring shoots when I stumbled upon your body laying in a field. You had a raging fever and you were hardly breathing. I didn't know what else to do."

"You carried me?"

"You were delirious but I was able to get you to stand and lean on me back to the cabin."

"I need to get out of here," I say. "I need to get back to the Safety Zone. They can give me a new Net there."

"If you try to go near the border without a Net the military will shoot you."

"What do you mean?"

"They'll think you're one of us."

"So you mean... I'm stuck here? Forever?"

"I didn't know what else to do. You would have died..."

"Then you should have left me to die. You should've... you should've..."

"Shh, you're hyperventilating. Here, drink some water."

The Tok Rebellion

"No. I need to get out of here. I need to..." I pull the covers off and swing my legs over the side of the bed but when I sit up I feel intensely dizzy and almost puke.

"Lay back down. You need water. Here. Drink."

She puts the glass to my lips and tilts a little water into my mouth sip by sip.

"It's going to be alright," she says. "I promise."

12

The next morning I wake up feeling stronger, more clear-headed. I'm able to sit up in bed. I stand, tentatively, and for a moment I feel nauseous as the blood rushes to my head, but it passes. I take a few steps and, finding them successful, try the door. It's unlocked.

Outside, the living room is small, rustic, centered around a wood-burning stove whose round metal smokestack is piped vertically up through the ceiling. Beside it sits a dining room table around which the father and daughter are seated.

The Tok Rebellion

"Morning," he says. "Would you like some breakfast?"

I nod my head.

The man pulls out a chair and I take a seat at the table. Chessed is sitting across from me. "Hey," I say.

"You're looking better," she says. Her eyes are wide and expressive. Her face is oval and luminous, highlighted by the curve of her upturned nose and strong cheekbones.

"How long was I out?" I ask.

"I found you seven days ago."

The father sets a plate in front of me and sits down next to me at the table.

"That's deer sausage, scrambled eggs and sourdough."

"Thank you," I say.

"My name is Geburah. That's Chessed, my daughter."

"It's nice to meet you. I'm Cassian." I cut into the dark sausage patty with my fork and venture a taste. It's rich, gamy, with a hint of sage. The flavors are almost too much for my weak stomach.

"Chessed found you in the woods. When she brought you back here you were on the brink of death. You're lucky to be alive."

"Thanks for that," I say.

"Would you like some bay laurel coffee?" Chessed asks.

"What's that?"

39

"It's a drink. We make it from roasted bay laurel nuts. It's hard to get real coffee up here but it tastes pretty similar."

"Sure, I'll take a cup."

She pours a cup of steaming black liquid from a percolator on the stovetop and places it in front of me.

"Cream?"

"No thanks."

"We don't know exactly what to do with you," Geburah says. He is a mountain of a man with shaggy black hair and a long grizzled beard. He's wearing a green plaid flannel with suspenders.

"Dad!"

"It has to be broached, Chessed. It's highly unusual to have an integrated in our midst. Or at least, formerly integrated."

I instinctively reach up and feel the sore sutured spot where my Net used to be. "Is that what you call us?"

"That's what you call our land, isn't it? 'Unintegrated Territory.' Territory just waiting to be reclaimed by the system."

"Look, I don't want to get into an ideological..."

"The world is ideological. Eventually, you have to get off the fence and decide what matters." Geburah looks at me with an intensity that I am unaccustomed to. People in my world had glazed-over, half-conscious expressions, distracted as they were by ads, bots, and

The Tok Rebellion

notifications. I look at my plate and poke at the eggs, silent.

Just then the front door comes open and a clattering of hooves can be heard on the hardwood floor.

"Chessed, how many times have I told you to shut the door all the way?"

"It's just Cedric, Dad. Don't get all grumpy."

A pink and black spotted pig eagerly trots up to my side, pushing its nose into my pant leg and grunting sweet innocent grunts.

"Leave him alone, Cedric," Chessed says, attempting to pull the little creature back. "He just wants your food."

"It's..."

"What?"

"No, it's just, I've never seen a pig before. I didn't realize how cute they are."

"You've never seen a pig before?"

"I mean, I knew they existed, of course. I know I've seen cartoon images of them. I must have seen a picture of one at some point... but no. I've, uh, never seen a pig before."

"In the integrated world people do not see where their food comes from," Geburah says from the kitchen sink, scrubbing dishes. "They are alienated from the entire process which connects them to nature."

"Go say hi to Cassian," Chessed says. "He's never seen a little pig before."

The curious hoofed fuzzball wriggles free from her grasp and comes oinking up to me, putting its front legs up on my thigh.

"Go on, you can pet him. He won't bite."

I scratch the creature behind its ears generating many grunts of approval from the affectionate pig.

"Chessed, not at the table," Geburah says.

"Come on, buddy, you gotta go back outside."

Chessed herds Cedric out the door and shuts it firmly behind him.

"You should get some more rest," Geburah says. "Chessed and I have a lot of work to do today."

"If it's alright with you, I'd kind of like to see your farm."

"Oh I'm sure you would, and make a break for it as soon as you see your chance."

"No, no. I wouldn't. I mean, Chessed said they'd shoot me, right? If I got too close to the border."

He appraises me with a stern gaze.

"Father, how many times have you said we needed help on the farm? God has answered your prayers with this young man."

Geburah scoffs. "This man hasn't done a decent day's work in his entire life."

"Please. Let me at least show him around. Tomorrow I can set him to work chopping wood if he has the strength for it."

The Tok Rebellion

"Take the pistol with you. If he starts to run, shoot him."

13

"These are the chickens," Chessed says, the gun sitting in a modern holster at her waist, incongruous with the rest of her homespun attire. "That's Betty. That one over there is Marg. Oh and that's Zeke," she says pointing to a rooster in the back of the chicken wire enclosure.

"What do you feed them?"

"See, there's a sack of meal over there. Go grab a scoop." I fish the plastic scoop out of the sack, carrying with it a heaping pile of the ground yellow grain. "Now what?"

The Tok Rebellion

"Just throw it in there," she says, pulling back a portion of the wire mesh.

I toss in the grain and the chickens flutter greedily around the meal.

"So they give you eggs?"

"Every day. C'mon. While they're distracted with the food." She leads me around the back of the coop where she slides a wooden hatch open. Reaching in shoulder deep she grasps something and when she pulls her arm back out she is holding a brown speckled egg. "See?"

Together we fill the basket.

"What do we do with the ones that have shit and feathers on them?"

"Just rinse them off. It's no big deal. You really have never lived on a farm before, have you?"

"Nope. Spent all my life in the city, basically."

"Is it true what they say about the girls there?"

"I don't know, what do they say?"

"That they're promiscuous."

"Promiscuous?"

"That they, you know, show their naked bodies online and play easy?"

"Oh, well, they definitely don't all show their naked bodies online."

"But the sex is casual, right?"

"Yes. There's nothing too special about it. Just something to do."

"Just something to do," she repeats. "Dad says the cities are filled with sin and ignorance. Ignorance of the human connection to God."

"Well, I guess I would call myself an atheist, agnostic maybe. I don't really believe in God," I say.

"You are very strange, Mr. Cassian."

"Why don't you show me the garden," I suggest, not wanting to get into a theological discussion with someone who has clearly been brainwashed by fundamentalist religion.

Geburah is not far off, clearing rocks from a field beyond the cabin and stacking them into a low wall. Chessed leads me to a tilled patch of earth, surrounded too by chicken wire. "The snows have only just melted. It's still early, but here you can see the asparagus coming up and the herbs are already showing signs of life. Rosemary, thyme, cilantro."

"How long have you lived out here?"

"I've always lived here. Even before the Great Reset."

"Reset?"

"That's right, I forgot, you call it the cyberpandemic, right?"

"Yes."

"I was fourteen. It changed everything."

"And what about your mother?" I regretted asking the question as soon as the words spilled out of my mouth.

"She died," she says in a clear but soft voice.

The Tok Rebellion

"I'm sorry. I... I shouldn't have asked that."

"It was during the Reset. She was coming home from the grocery store. Everything went offline and a car hit her. It lost its connection to the maps or whatever and was just careening down the road."

"I'm sorry. That's horrible. They're programmed not to do that. I wonder why..."

"I don't know. But I do know that God took her for a reason and it will all make sense in the end."

"Are there other people like you out here? Is there a town?"

"Of course there are others like us. Nevada City is the nearest town. That's where we go to trade and sell food, but there are people like us spread out all over the State of Jefferson."

"And what is your goal?"

"Goal?"

"I mean what are you trying to accomplish out here?"

"We just want to live. Isn't that enough?"

14

After the tour, Chessed takes me back to my room to recover. "I know this life probably seems strange and backward to you, but I promise it's a good one. There are things more important than just the material. If you need anything, I'll be out in the yard."

"Thanks," I say.

I spend the afternoon lying in bed, fidgeting and writhing with dopamine withdrawals. I was used to countless notifications, checking things, reminders, emails. Without a constant feed of distraction it felt like there was this underlying anxious urge in my body

The Tok Rebellion

gnawing away at my bones. Was boredom like delirium tremens? Could it kill you?

I distract myself by plotting my escape. It won't be too hard to gain the trust of these two, I think. Especially the girl. All I have to do is play along with the farm work until I find a moment alone. Then I would run. Which way? Now that is a problem. I have no idea how I got here. But I know I can't be that far from Auburn. And even if I do manage to get near the city, how do I convince the Security Forces that I'm not a fundamentalist spy?

My face scan, of course! Even without my net, they'll be able to see I'm a registered citizen. That is if they don't shoot me on the spot. Them or the militias. It's a narrow chance but it's better than spending my life in this psychotic religious cult.

The afternoon wears on into evening and the light turns orange and slanted in my room. I hear my captors come back inside, presumably done with their work for the day. I hear their muffled voices, sparse chit chat, and then there is another sound. It sounds more like recorded voices, changing intermittently like they would in a feed. Curious, I rouse myself from bed and enter the main room of the cabin. Propped up on the table is an old phone, the kind my parents had before the Net. On it, Geburah and Chessed are watching videos.

"I'll be at the Yreka market this Saturday selling solar battery packs and charging cables. I accept cash and trades and if you're in a dire situation, I can work something out for you." Geburah reaches forward and swipes up. The video of the man selling solar panels is replaced by a woman in front of a shelf of books.

"Rebel forces in Coeur d'Alene have liberated the city from government occupiers, unifying Northern Idaho under rebel control. Montana remains divided with the government still controlling most of the large cities. Airstrikes continue in Northern Jefferson with sixteen reported dead in Ashland."

"What are you watching?" I ask, joining them at the table.

"It's TikTok," Chessed says. "It's what we use to communicate."

"TikTok? Wasn't that banned like fifteen years ago?"

"There are still some phones left with it downloaded," Geburah says. "It cost me almost as much as this farm."

"But how do you receive a signal?"

"Over the years we have recovered and restored old cell towers, hooking them up to solar arrays. Someone found an old server warehouse in Oregon and hacked the app to run from there. In the beginning, after the Great Reset, everyone felt so isolated, but now it's like we are all connected. Every day the service area increases and more rebels are brought into the fold."

The Tok Rebellion

"Does the government know that you're using this?"

"Not as far as we know," he says, eyeing me suspiciously.

He swipes up again and a hooded figure fills the screen.

"Rebels, patriots, fellow humans. This morning at 10 am a bomb was detonated in the boardroom of Rayheed Marthon killing ten board members and the CEO. Over the past 50 years, Rayheed Marthon has supplied the government with weapons to oppress and murder countless people around the globe and recently the government has turned those weapons against the citizens of its own country. We have lost thousands to the government bombing campaigns. Rayheed Marthon has profited from the pain and death of so many people and today they have paid for their sins. Today I placed that bomb in their headquarters and took the lives of those who have killed so many. Their slaying was swift and brutal. The elites must know that they can no longer profit off death without reaping what they sow."

"Is that... Tok?" I ask.

"Yes," Geburah says. "He is our leader."

"Fuck. This is your leader? This terrorist? He just killed eleven people for Christ's sake. Isn't that a sin to you people?"

"Tok is a messenger of God. If God has judged that these men must die, then it will be so. You don't need faith to see that the world will be better off without these people in it."

"Yeah, but there's got to be a better way to solve this than killing them. That's horrible."

"No. The destruction they wreak on innocent people is horrible. They lived in the nucleus of a system that thrives on the blood of the poor and defenseless. They created a system of violence and within it violence is the only language they understand."

"I'm sorry but that line of thinking is deranged. You're telling me you believe in God and then go cheering on this mass murderer terrorist. Can't you see the disconnect?"

"You've been in the system for a long time," Geburah says. "You're programmed to react this way."

"Well from my perspective, you're the ones who are brainwashed."

Geburah stands abruptly and puts his hand on his pistol, strapped in a leather holster under his arm.

"Father please, it's alright," Chessed says.

"Oh sure," I say. "Either I agree with you or you shoot me. Really rational ideology."

"I know it's hard for you to understand," Chessed says. "It pains me to know that those people were killed, but I also know that there is good in this world and those people were trying to stamp it out. It may seem cruel, but you haven't experienced what we have.

The Tok Rebellion

You haven't seen all the senseless death." She looks up at me with a profound sadness in her eyes.

"Look, I'm sorry. This is getting heated," I say. "It's a lot to take in."

15

Later, Chessed brings me dinner in my room.

"I'm sorry about all that," I say.

"It's okay. We're from different worlds. You don't understand." She puts down a plate of potatoes and asparagus on the bedside table and takes a seat on my bed.

"I mean, this is tense. I don't know if I can ever come to understand you. Religion, God, terrorism? How could I possibly understand all that?"

"To us, you are the terrorists. There is power in words. Perhaps they are the most powerful."

"Then why take me in? Why save me?"

"Wouldn't you have done the same if you found me dying on the street in your city?"

I turn away and look out the window into the darkness beyond, ashamed to tell her the truth, that there are many people dying on the streets of my city and I've never done anything to help them.

"I know this is hard for you. This isn't an ideal situation for either of us, but I know that everything happens for a reason. Finding you was fate and not knowing what will happen doesn't mean there isn't a plan."

16

I am roused from my restless slumber by a soft nuzzle to my ear. The pig, Cedric, has gotten into my room. "Hey, hey little guy stop it... hahaha. Okay, that's enough!" I pat the pig on the head, gather a blanket around me to protect from the chill morning air and wander into the living room.

"Coffee?" Geburah asks.

"Um, sure."

"Not the real stuff. Bay laurel coffee. There's some chemical in there though. Kind of like caffeine. Gives it a kick."

I sit down at the table with him.

The Tok Rebellion

"Hey, I'm sorry about last night. I didn't mean to..."

"You and I have our differences and they are deeper than differences of character. It is a cultural and spiritual schism that goes back many generations. We cannot expect to understand one another in a single night."

"True."

"Put it out of your mind for now. There's work to do today."

17

The chopping block is a weathered smitten stump bleached white-gray from the sun. Steam rises in whorls from the inchoate grasses pushing themselves up from the cold earth. I am wearing one of Geburah's jackets. It's two sizes too big.

"Have you ever chopped wood before?"

"Umm, you know it feels like I should have at some point but no, I don't think so."

"It's pretty self-explanatory. Use the wedge and the hammer to break up the bigger pieces. The axe is over there. Let me know when you finish that pile. Then we can have some breakfast."

The Tok Rebellion

He wanders off into the yard never taking me from his sight. The pistol is strapped, threatening, under his arm.

I pick a smaller cylinder of wood and balance it on the stump. The axe feels foreign in my hands, more accustomed to typing on projected keyboards than manual labor. I take a swing and only graze the side of the log, chipping off a disappointing sliver. I swing again, this time hitting it near the center, but instead of the wood splitting in two, the axe gets lodged in the grain.

I have to hold the log down with my foot, angling the axe back and forth to extract it. I try again and get the same result. The log doesn't seem big enough to warrant the wedge and hammer so I try a different approach. With more force, I imagine myself swinging through the log into the stump below. Success. A section of wood goes flying off with a satisfying crack.

I find the chopping to be addictive. Splitting the rough logs into manageable burnable chunks and watching my progress as the stack grows. The knotty pieces give me a particular pleasure when I strike them into incongruent wavy shapes. Soon I am losing myself in the work.

At some point, I look up and see Geburah and Chessed watching me, smiling and giggling respectively.

"Where'd you learn to swing an axe?" she calls. "The technology factory?"

"What?" I call back, leaning on the axe handle.

"Nothing," she says.

"She means you look goofy," Geburah clarifies.

"I chopped all that wood there," I say, gesturing to my pile.

"That's all the wood you chopped? You've been at it so long I thought you must be hiding it behind the house."

"Yeah, yeah, yeah. Okay."

"C'mon. We're getting hungry. It's time for breakfast."

18

Later that day I'm still chopping when I see a man on horseback approaching along the driveway. Chessed goes to greet him and when he swings himself off the horse, he embraces her and kisses her on the mouth.

I'm surprised to feel a pang of jealousy shoot through my heart. He is tall and handsome with a cowboy hat tilted over his left eye. It's like witnessing a live anachronism, a cigarette ad from my grandparents' generation set into motion. Geburah joins them and shakes hands with the newcomer. They're at a distance and I can't make out what they're saying but I notice them gesturing at me. The man shoots a concerned look in my direction.

I lower my gaze and resume chopping. Through surreptitious glances, I watch them as they talk and then proceed as a group indoors. I am left alone outside with nothing but the dense, dark boundary of the forest on all sides. As the thought of running crosses my mind, I catch a glimpse of Geburah through the cabin window. He has me locked in his gaze and I feel as though he has read my mind. Sheepish, I return to my task, wondering who this new stranger is and what the three of them are discussing over the table.

19

The man has gone and in the afternoon Chessed is tasked with taking me to fetch water. We each carry two empty five-gallon water jugs. She leads me into the dappled light of the forest along a moss-lined path.

"Who was that guy?" I ask.

"That's Turner. We're engaged to be married later this year."

"Ahh, I see. Handsome guy, nice catch."

"He's a lieutenant in the militias. I'm so proud of him. He's been at the front lines in Auburn holding off the security forces. General Logan says he's got a great tactical mind."

"General Logan?"

"He's in charge of all the militias in the Sierra Region."

We march on through the oaks and pines, the trail first ascending, then descending back down a hill into a hollow beyond.

"Watch out for that plant," she says, pointing to a shrubby outgrowth with the toe of her shoe. "It's poison oak. Do they have that where you're from?"

"Not that I know of," I say. "Do you know all the plants?"

"Oh yes, at least the ones around here."

"What's this?" I say, patting the rough, roped bark of a tree trunk.

"That's easy. That's a Jeffrey pine. They're all over here."

"What about that one?" I say, pointing to a spindly tree with broad bright green leaves.

"Bigleaf maple," she responds. "It's got the biggest leaves of any maple in the world."

"Appropriately named," I say.

We follow the trail into a lush gully where the sound of water can be heard trickling.

"Holy crap, this place is beautiful."

She laughs.

"What?"

"You just have a funny way of talking. Holy crap."

"That's actually the nice way of saying it."

The Tok Rebellion

"It's just kind of funny to imagine. A holy piece of crap. But really it's true. Everything is holy."

We venture down to the edge of a little stream, ethereal and fairy-like in the tumble-down mossy rocks. She steps along the bank up to a crystal clear pool, above which the source comes bubbling out of a cascade of boulders. She unscrews the jug and, leaning over the pool, places it under the gurgling flow of the stream.

"This is where you get your water? Aren't you afraid of bacteria?"

She laughs again. "This water has been filtered through the pores of the earth for hundreds of years, something your filtration systems don't even come close to replicating.

"Yeah but like, couldn't there be bird poop on the rocks or heavy metals in the water or something?"

"You're crazy. You would rather have dead chemically treated sanitized water than this fresh living pure water straight from the earth."

"I mean, you can get sick from drinking bad water, right?"

"I've been drinking from this spring since I was a child. Try some."

"Try some? How?"

"Just stick your head under there, dummy."

She moves aside, making a little room for me to kneel next to the spring.

"Go on. You're not going to get sick. I promise."

I place my hands on two slippery rocks and lean in, turning my head sideways to meet the water at its source. Ice cold droplets splash on my face as I draw mouthful after mouthful of the cool sweet water down my throat. I pause for a breath before going in for one more gulp when my hand slips and I go tumbling into the pool.

Shocked and chilled to the bone, I pull my face out of the water to find Chessed doubled over with laughter. "How was it?" she asks.

"Surprisingly good," I say, shaking the water from my dripping locks. "I'm alive."

"C'mon, you can dry off on the walk home. You may as well make yourself useful while you're in there and fill the other jugs.

20

My shoulders are already burning when we're only halfway out of the valley. I set the jugs down on the trail and take a few deep breaths. "Tired out already?" she asks.

"Heh heh, I just need a breather," I say, heaving air into my lungs.

"I can see why my dad wasn't worried about you overpowering me out here," she says.

"How long are you planning on escorting me at gunpoint, anyway?"

"Till we can trust you, I guess."

"So I'm basically your slave then."

"Am I a slave to my father? Are we slaves to the land? You have to work in order to live, there's no way around it."

"I never worked this hard in the city."

"Someone somewhere was doing the work so that you could live. Farm workers, people in factories."

"Machines do a lot of that now."

"I know the myth of your culture. That one day the machines will make the machines and robots will do all the work and there will be a paradise of abundance for all. You forget that somewhere there is an earth beneath it all and that the robots come from the earth, big gaping holes where they strike the rare metals from the soil. Where has your myth gotten you? Are you truly so advanced that you can forsake your Mother?"

21

Back at the cabin, Geburah explains to me that tomorrow is a market day. I am to help with the loading and accompany them into town to work the farm stand. He warns me that if I make any sign of trying to run, he has no qualms about shooting me dead where I stand.

Dinner is a soup prepared by Chessed. Potatoes, celery, wild carrot, onions, garlic. She has simmered a beef bone in the broth and the tallow sits in little yellow droplets, glistening in the electric light of the cabin.

"How do you power these lights?" I ask.

Nate Lemcke

"There's a solar panel back beyond where you were chopping wood. It's not much but it's enough to run the lights for a few hours every night."

"And to charge the phone," Chessed says.

After dinner, we watch TikTok, consumed by the little glowing screen on the table, as Geburah scrolls through the assorted faces of the State of Jefferson and beyond. Herbalists, trappers, soldiers, midwives, craftsmen. These are the people who never accepted the Notes. The people who never had NeuralNets implanted. These seemingly regular backwoods kinds of people were the ones the government wanted to integrate. They are the far-right fascists I had heard so much about in the news.

The thing is, they don't seem nearly like the terrorists the news made them out to be. They just seem like people who want to live their lives. Of course, I knew that the videos were somewhat curated. Of course, no one is going to show their worst sides on camera, but it's not like they are trying to convince anyone of anything. This footage wasn't even reaching the National Safety Zones. They are talking to each other authentically and without pretense.

There is no new video from Tok and after about forty-five minutes Geburah puts the phone away somewhere in his room. Chessed selects a book from the small bookshelf and reclines on a couch next to the fireplace.

The Tok Rebellion

I take a few pieces of wood that I had chopped earlier and stack them onto the gentle blaze. I can't remember the last time I saw a fire. We had e-cigs, electric stoves, and central heating. The mesmerizing glow of a flame was foreign to me. I sit there watching it crackle for a while before asking Chessed what she's reading.

"*To the Lighthouse*," she says.

"Who wrote it?"

I can hear Geburah snort in disapproval from somewhere back in the kitchen.

"You don't know who wrote *To the Lighthouse*?" she says, smiling in disbelief.

"No, should I?"

"She's only one of the greatest authors of all time."

"Who?"

"Virginia Woolf."

I shrug, ignorant.

"Jeez, they really don't teach you anything in the Safety Zones, do they?"

"I mean, I learned to write code."

"And what good is that doing you now?"

"Good point. What's it about?"

"It's about war. And the impermanence of things. And how the things you seek are never the same once you attain them."

"Heavy stuff."

"But she writes it in this stylized intricate way, almost like it's a puzzle that you have to figure out."

"I'll have to read it when you're done."

"Here," she says, handing the book to me. "I've only read it a dozen times."

"Thanks," I say.

I lay on the rug reading in front of the fire and about an hour later there is a small electric beep and the lights go out. "Well that's all the electricity for today," Geburah says. "We should get to bed. We have an early start tomorrow."

22

I am awoken while it's still dark out by the sound of Geburah cooking breakfast in the kitchen. Chessed is already carting various crafts out of her room and out the front door. I sit down at the table and Geburah serves me a plate of eggs and more venison sausage. "Come sit down, honey," he says on Chessed's return journey. We eat a quick breakfast and I pile the finished plates in the sink. "Don't worry about the dishes," Geburah says. "I need your help loading the truck."

It's an old Toyota pickup. Geburah has backed it up near the entrance to the cabin. He passes me sacks of potatoes from the root cellar that I heave into the bed. "Careful," he says. "I don't want any bruised potatoes."

After the potatoes we load sacks of chestnuts, walnuts, and dried persimmons. I nestle in a crate of blackberry preserves. Meanwhile Chessed packs her wares behind the seats in the cab.

With the truck fully loaded and a tarp secured over the bed, we pile in, Geburah driving, me in the passenger seat, and Chessed sandwiched between us, legs pressed against mine to avoid the gear shifter. She's wearing a sage green cotton dress and an old Carhartt with the hood up to protect her from the cold.

Geburah fires up the ignition and the engine roars to life and soon we are bouncing down the rocky driveway into the paling dawn.

"Where do you get the gas for this?" I ask, remembering that cars once ran on such a substance.

"There's a refinery in Wyoming that the rebels seized early in the war. Most of the gas comes from there. You have to remember, most of the oil-producing land is in rebel territory. A lot of it these days is cut with ethanol from bootleggers up in the mountains. It's cheaper."

We reach a point in the two-track driveway where brush and branches are piled over it in the woods. Geburah slows the car to a halt and Chessed pushes me to get out of the car. "C'mon, help me," she says and together we drag the tree branches out of the way,

The Tok Rebellion

puffs of respiration rising in the headlights. We clear the road and hop back into the cab. Geburah drives on.

"Should we cover it back up?"

"It will be fine for today," he says. Soon the driveway ends and we pull onto a wider dirt road.

"Early on in the war, the militias blew up all the highways going into and coming out of the State of Jefferson," Geburah explains, unprompted. "The only way to get around now is the old back roads. Besides, it's safer that way."

I watch the horizon growing orange out my window as the road turns steeper and rockier. Geburah slows the car and shifts into a lower gear. His daughter presses her legs against mine to make room for the shifter and a little tingle of sensation shoots up my leg where she brushes against me. Something in my heart stirs and I am surprised by the unexpected intimacy of this cramped car ride.

Through switchbacks and turns I am carted further into a wild land. I see deer gathered on the side of the road and squirrels fleeing from the crunch of the truck tires. Birds flit among the branches and through a gap in the trees the first ray of warm sunlight comes beaming across my face.

23

The main street is abuzz with activity as vendors set up tents to sell their wares and eager shoppers already start to peruse the assorted sellers' stalls. Car batteries, pickles, flashlights, extension cords, crates of old books, dried fish, smoked jerky, woven baskets, a whole stand of firearms. It's like an apocalyptic flea market.

People ride through on horseback or gather with their families around a hot fry bread tent. There are people with tattoos, and satchels, and dreadlocks, and beards tucked into their belts. The diversity assembled

The Tok Rebellion

here is unlike anything one encounters in the National Safety Zones.

Geburah, Chessed, and I erect the poles and tent covering for our stall at the end of a row of other vendors. I help prop up a couple old folding tables, the plastic kind with awkward brown metal tubing underneath that snaps into place. On top we set out the goods that Geburah, Chessed, and their modest farm have produced.

I'm not allowed to interact with the customers. I hang back on the tailgate of the truck, weighing out potatoes and nuts at Geburah's command. The most popular item is Chessed's honey. I didn't see her pack it. She must have put it in the truck before I awoke. People came specifically to our stall to ask for it.

"Do you have any more of that blackberry honey? We ran out after two weeks. I better get four jars this time."

This primitive economy runs off of old United States paper money and coins. None has been printed since we switched to Notes in 2034 and most of the bills Geburah and Chessed receive are crumpled and ripped. A crisp bill, they say, is worth double.

Geburah explains to me that after the Great Reset, the scarcity of cash made it the perfect currency. Coins you could find on the street became worth ten times as much overnight. None like them would ever be coined again.

Chessed sells hand-sewn scrubbing pads with burlap on one side and a softer fabric with vintage designs on the other. She has cloth napkins with embroidered trees and forest creatures. Geburah acquiesces to customer demands with a courteous salesmanship I did not expect from him.

Shadows on the street shorten then grow longer. The thoroughfare becomes increasingly crowded then begins to dwindle. By mid afternoon we have nearly sold out.

"I'm going to do some shopping before the market shuts down," Geburah says. "Can you two man the fort while I'm away?"

Chessed nods.

"If he even thinks of running away, scream out, so everyone can hear, that he's an integrated spy." Then he looks me dead in the eye. "The only thing these people hate more than security forces are spies."

He takes a handful of cash from the lock box and leaves us under the tent to handle any remaining customers.

"How often do you come here?" I ask.

"There are farmer's markets every week, but this big market only happens once a month. It brings out people from all over the mountains, even as far as Shasta."

"Shasta. I've never been there. I hear a lot about it in the news."

The Tok Rebellion

"It's sad. That's where a lot of the bombing takes place. They used to have a spring there. Probably one of the most magical springs in the world..."

"Chessed!" a girl cries out and comes running up to the stand.

"Hey, Amy! I was wondering when you would show up. How did you do today?"

"Eh, I did alright. It looks like you guys sold out! Who's this? A new farmhand?" Amy is blonde with two braids, one draped over each shoulder. She is wearing worn-in black leather boots with jeans and a flannel.

"It's a long story. I'll tell you later. His name is Cassian."

"Hi, Cassian. You look so clean cut. What are you, from the safety zones or something?" she asks with piercing blue eyes.

"Something like that."

"Are you coming to ecstatic dance tonight?" she asks Chessed.

"I don't know. My father probably wants to get home before dark."

"Boo," Amy says, affecting an exaggerated pout. "You never come anymore."

"There's been a lot of work on the farm."

"Yeah, yeah, yeah. Your friends are important too, you know."

24

After we break down the tent and pack everything into the truck, Geburah offers to take us out to dinner.

"You two worked hard today. I appreciate it."

We walk up the sidewalk of the main street. It is lined with pioneer-era buildings like something from a time gone by.

"Did you all build these?" I ask.

"Ha!" Geburah ejaculates. "These are from the Gold Rush, son. A lot of these buildings are well over a hundred years old." He pulls open the door of what looks like an old hotel and I follow Chessed inside. The wooden sign above the door reads "The Exchange."

The Tok Rebellion

The interior is lit by candlelight. Murky purple wallpaper with intricate designs fades into the gloom of the bar. A waiter leads us into a dining room where he sits us at a table covered with a white tablecloth.

"This is the nicest restaurant in town," Chessed half whispers to me.

"It used to be a brothel back in the day," Geburah says.

"You mean before the Reset?" I ask.

"Back in the 1800's," he says. "The wild west."

I take a look at the paper menu. Someone has gone through the trouble of writing by hand all the dishes, descriptions, and prices. Printers and the electricity to run them must be hard to come by.

Stuffed rabbit saddle. Hanger steak with charred spring asparagus. Wood-fired trout.

The waiter, an old man with a bushy mustache and thinning hair comes by and asks for drinks. I stick with water. Chessed orders an iced tea. For Geburah it's scotch, I can't make out the name, Boonahaven or something, neat.

"I didn't know you drank," I say. "I thought it might be against your religion or something."

"I imagine you think we go to a little white picket fence church every Sunday and thump the Bible."

"I mean..."

"You'll find that the people of Jefferson are far more varied than the stereotypes your news pumps out would suggest."

"Why do you call it that anyway? The State of Jefferson"

"Jefferson believed that a society of small, self-sufficient family farms would ensure a democratic and self-governing nation. He disliked big banks and advocated for an agricultural based society. He thought this would make us a stronger country."

"Jefferson, that's the guy who wrote the Declaration of Independence, right?"

"Look Chessed, he does have some learning after all."

The waiter comes back with our drinks and asks for our orders. Chessed orders the trout with a side of brussel sprouts. Not wanting to put my host out, I order one of the cheapest things on the menu.

"No, he's not having that," Geburah says. "Have a steak with me, I insist."

"Okay, I'll take the steak," I say.

"How would you like it cooked?"

"Medium rare."

"Good man," Geburah says. "I'll have the same thing. Thank you."

The food is delicious. Geburah orders another scotch. Near the end of the meal a group of boisterous men walk through the restaurant.

"Geburah! Hey Geburah!"

The Tok Rebellion

"Give me a moment," he says, wiping his mouth and standing up to greet the men. They are burly like him. Farmer types. Overalls, big boots, and stained jeans. Scotch in hand, Geburah slaps one of the men on the back and joins in their conversation.

"This is good," Chessed says. "Those are my dad's friends. I think if we play this right he'll probably let us go to ecstatic dance."

"What is ecstatic dance?"

"C'mon," she says, getting up and pulling me by the hand.

"Dad, can I show Cassian ecstatic dance?"

"That will be fine, sweetheart. Meet me back here at the bar when you're done."

25

We go out into the night, her skipping, me following close behind up the lantern-lit street.

People mingle about outside restaurants and bars. The city is alive with post-market excitement. Chessed leads me down two blocks to a building from which drifts an upbeat clamorous tempo.

She pays for us a cash fee at the door to a person decked out in crow feathers and heavy eye makeup. We are in an antechamber where a small bar is selling beverages. Inside the next set of double doors lights flash and a crowd dances to a live band.

"There's electricity in here," I say.

The Tok Rebellion

"They run a generator. It's one of the biggest events in town."

"It's like a rave?"

"Kind of. There are rules though. No talking and dance however your heart desires."

She pulls me into the dance hall by the wrist and navigates us through the revelers to a spot near the stage. Four musicians are playing strings and drums in what I can only describe as some fusion of tribal and folk music. Chessed outstretches her arms and sways back and forth to the beat. Around me people are dancing in such uninhibited ways I can't help but be embarrassed for them. Nobody back in the city would ever dance like this. Heads thrown back, shaking like they're having an exorcism. People crawling and rolling around on the floor. One old man in tights is spinning around the dance floor and gesturing wildly to some unseen god above.

Not sure what to do, I attempt to pump my fist in the air, but it feels off so I settle for moving my shoulders and bending my knees. Dancing was never my strong suit.

I feel a tap on my shoulder. I turn around and it's the girl from the market, Amy. She's changed outfits and now she's wearing a mid-thigh length black pleather skirt, fishnet stockings, and a tank top. She waves hi and I wave back. Using both hands she mimics holding a sphere and moves it back and forth to the time of the music. She crouches low, circling her hands around this imaginary ball. Then without warning she tosses it up into the air.

I look up following its invisible trajectory, waiting a moment before miming catching it. Then I start acting like I'm playing with the ball, moving it between my legs, passing it behind my back, and rolling it over my shoulders before chucking it deep into the recesses of the crowd.

At this point Amy is letting the music course through her. Her eyes are closed and I turn back to Chessed. Making eye contact, I raise and lower my shoulders, trying to make a funny expression.

Chessed shakes her head. She takes each of my hands in her own and begins to lead me, swaying back and forth. Holding eye contact, she takes us down, bouncing to the rhythm. She spins, placing her back against me and tracing with my hand the length of her side. She is pulling me into the flow of the music and guiding me with her body. I feel clumsy and self-conscious but eventually I catch some semblance of a beat working through me and moving with her. She spins again and pulls herself in close, staring into my eyes. For a moment it seems we are lost in time, then the song switches and she is back to dancing on her own.

26

Outside in the alley Amy is smoking a joint. She asks Chessed if she wants any. "Sure," she says. I'm surprised to see her take a drag.

"Do you smoke, city boy?" Amy asks.

Chessed passes the joint to me and I suck on the paper, still wet with her mouth, inhaling a lungful of harsh skunky weed.

"Where'd you find this guy anyways?"

"I told you I'd tell you later."

"She saved my life," I say.

"She's good at that," Amy says. "How'd she save yours?"

"I was lost. I left the city one night. I guess I got sick. She found me in the woods."

"So you are from the Safety Zones. I knew it! Are you integrated?" She tries to pull back my hair and look at the side of my head.

"I was."

"Shit Chessed. This guy could be dangerous."

"He's fine," Chessed says, her voice firm.

"He could be a spy or something."

"He's fine."

Amy eyes me warily.

"Look, I know I don't belong here. But I didn't really belong back there either. So where am I supposed to be?"

"C'mon," Chessed says. "They're starting the next set."

27

After the show we emerge from the dance hall. "Oh my lord, that was so good. I needed that," Chessed says, spinning into the empty street with her arms outstretched.

"You guys wanna come back to my place?" Amy asks. "A bunch of friends are meeting there."

"Yeah okay."

"What about your dad?" I ask.

"He'll still be drinking. When he meets up with those friends they usually close down the bar."

Back into the night and the quaint two story steep roofed houses and the twinkling stars, Amy leads us down winding side streets until we arrive at a slim ramshackle house. The windows are filled with the shifting silhouettes of gathered strangers. She unlatches an old chain link gate and leads us up a cracked and slanted sidewalk to her home.

Inside are the likes of poets, soldiers, and revolutionaries. I am introduced to a few drunken acquaintances. "This is Robert. He's writing a manifesto on the consequences of material realism. Oh, and this is my brother, Jack."

"Let me know if you need anything to drink, buddy. A friend of Amy's is a friend of mine."

"Over here, this is Andrew. He just got back from the front lines."

"What about Turner?" I ask. "Is he here?"

"No. He's out fighting." Chessed sits me at a little corner table next to the soldier, too young to be so grim.

"Hey," I say.

He grunts.

"What's... what's the war like?" I ask.

"What are you, a narc?" he spits.

"No, no. I'm just, I don't know. I really don't know what it's like for you guys."

"It's hell," he says.

"What did you do before?"

"Before the war? I was thirteen. My dad got killed in a government raid. I've been fighting ever since then."

The Tok Rebellion

"I'm sorry," I say.

"What's your story anyway? You don't seem like you're from around here."

"To be honest, I'm not. I'm from the cities."

"So you're the fuckin' enemy."

"I mean, I was. I didn't know I was."

"Wanna beer?" he asks.

He goes to the kitchen and returns with a glass bottle. "Jack makes it himself. Grows the hops and everything." A hand-drawn label is glued to the side of the bottle. "Jack's Timberjack Lager."

I take a swig. The citrusy crispness is followed by a slight homebrew aftertaste.

"You know they moved a family into my old home? A whole fuckin integrated family."

"That sucks," I say.

"I used to live in Auburn, before the security forces took it. I sneaked past enemy lines one night just to see for myself. Our old couch, dining room table, just piled in the front yard like garbage. Inside this family was painting the walls, just laughing and having a good time. I wanted to kill all of them."

28

Chessed is driving and I am stuck in the middle, crammed in next to Geburah who is glassy-eyed and smelling of whiskey. The dusty road seems to be created, sucked in, and destroyed by the headlights while above us a half moon shines, foretelling neither joy nor disaster.

Our driver eases the truck into third and I mash my bony knees into Geburah's massive thigh to make room. "When I was a young man, I didn't think anything was sacred either," he muses to me and to the night. "I was a hotshot. I would fight fires in the summer and spend my winters chasing women. The

The Tok Rebellion

world to me was something to be enjoyed. Something to be consumed. Then I met her mother. I was on a fire up in Idaho. We had it mostly contained and the crew was just waiting for word to be sent home.

"There was time to kill so I went off on my own to find a stream I had seen a few days before. I wanted to cool off. Take a dip. But when I got down there, a woman was standing in the pool. I came stomping, causing a ruckus no doubt, through the underbrush and when I reached the stream, there she was, wading waist deep. The most beautiful woman I had ever seen. I was ashamed at her nakedness. I felt horrible for intruding, but she beckoned me in. She told me later she sensed a softness in me. A softness that I did not know then that I possessed.

"After that day in the creek, I knew I wanted to be with her for the rest of my life. I invited her back to California with me. We bought the cabin together. She showed me the magic in the plants, the animals, the soil. She showed me everything was alive with God. Even her passing had a hint of God in it."

"Father..."

"No, I believe this. I believe this to be the case. We are all of us dying and we are all of us alive. Life is an infinite series of intermeshed paradoxes. Your mother's soul leaving this world was just as much a part of it as the sun setting or the rain falling. It's not fate. It's an inexorable unfolding all of which arises from and points to God. She taught me that. Your mother. And she would want you to believe it too."

29

I am fetching water. I am chopping wood. I am always under the watch of Chessed or her father. It does not escape me that I have left one surveillance state for another. My hands are calloused. My back is sore. I help Geburah plow the fields. We plant corn and squash and beans, sisters, he says, as old as time immemorial.

There is a satisfaction in a day's labor that programming and marketing never gave me. The sense of having completed something meaningful. Having contributed in a real way to my own survival and to the survival of those around me. There is a connection to the land I never felt in the city. Indeed, "the land" had no such numinous quality as it does now. I start to see the infinitesimal connections. I start to see that I cannot be separated from it.

One day Geburah goes out to buy gas, loading the back of the Toyota with red fuel canisters. Chessed asks me to accompany her to the spring. She forgets the gun. She is talking, walking ahead of me, not realizing I am straggling behind. I linger at the driveway, the empty driveway leading to the road and civilization.

I see myself running, navigating downhill toward Auburn, skirting around the barricades, the same way I had come in, finding someone who would listen to my story, showing them my scar. It would all be so easy. My friends, my parents worried sick, my old apartment (probably rented to someone new by now.) A new Net. Emails, messages, PornBots, immunity updates...

"Cassian?" I hear Chessed call out.

Another day. I can do it another day.

I'm stronger now. My skin is tan and creased from the sun. I am growing a beard. With the clothes they bought me, I am looking more and more like one of the rebels. The days spent with Chessed are like a balm to my soul. I am beginning to believe I have such a cumbersome thing.

She takes me out to forage spring mushrooms, flushed after a spell of rain.

The Tok Rebellion

"Mushrooms are a relatively guilt-free way of consuming the biosphere. It feels like you're pulling a whole organism out of the earth," she says, extracting a golden chanterelle. "But really it's just the fruit. The main part of the mushroom lives underground. It's like if an apple tree lived completely beneath the surface of the earth and only popped up its apples.

"Although the concept of guilt-free shouldn't really concern you. Everything is always dying and eating and feeding everything else. The idea of individual species is a materialist myth."

To Chessed, materialism was like the Antichrist. "Scientific materialism," she would say, "has stripped the sacred from the world." We gather wood ear, yellow boletes, and fat velvety porcinis.

"Porcini means 'little pig,'" she explains as we head back to the cabin.

"You mean like Cedric?" I ask.

"Yes, exactly like Cedric."

"Maybe that's what I'll call you. My little porcini."

"Oh, shut up," she says, trying to push me off the trail.

"My fat little piggy," I say, tickling her until she's doubled over with laughter.

"Get your hands off my fiancée you integrated piece of shit," I hear a voice say. It's Turner. He's storming down the path towards us.

I put my hands up. "I'm sorry. I didn't mean anything by it. I swear."

He lunges at me, tobacco-stained spittle flying from his mouth, and plants his fist into my jaw, knocking me backward onto the ground. "What the fuck is this?" he screams, fuming. "You're going on little play dates with this liberal scum now? Answer me!"

"Turner, it was nothing. You are being ridiculous."

"I don't want to see you alone with that man ever again or I'll fuckin' kill him. I'll fuckin' kill him, do you understand me?"

30

I am in my room, Chessed in hers. My jaw is bruised and smarting. Outside, Turner is yelling at Geburah. I can't make out everything they're saying. "Wedding...", "daughter...", "shouldn't be on this farm." I risk a peek out the window. Turner is gesticulating wildly. Geburah, a head taller than him, is standing motionless. Eventually Turner takes his horse and leaves and I can hear Geburah in Chessed's room conversing with her.

It's my turn. Geburah asks me to join him in the kitchen. "Your behavior toward my daughter has been inappropriate."

Nate Lemcke

"But I-."

"Please. I never should have left you alone with her. She is an engaged woman, do you understand that? Her heart is sworn to someone else. You cannot violate the sanctity of that bond. From now on you will be working with me alone. You will not speak to my daughter other than for what is absolutely necessary. Have I made myself clear?"

"Yes, sir," I say, dejected, head bowed.

"Chessed is more sacred to me than this farm, than my own life. Do not risk what is best for her for your own temporary amusement. I know where you come from. Women are merely things to you. My daughter is not one of your city girls to be 'hooked up' with."

"I wasn't trying..."

"You have overstepped your role here. Tomorrow we'll move you to the shed out back. It was inappropriate of me to have you in the same house with my daughter for so long."

31

Geburah moves some tools around, extracts an old futon mattress out from under a number of boxes and clears a place for it on the plywood floor. I hold my bundle of clothes in my arms. "We both know that now that you're outside of the house you can run away. I don't care anymore. It would save me a heap of trouble. Man to man, I trust that if you decide to leave, you will not tell the security forces about our cabin, about our life up here. I'm asking you for Chessed's sake. This land is everything to her." His eyes are pleading, intense.

I nod. His gaze lingers on me for a moment before he shuts the shed door behind him.

32

I think about life back home daily, but something compels me to stay. Just a little longer, I tell myself. Now that I can leave whenever I want, some of the pressure has been taken off. I stay because I feel something I can't put my finger on. Something I never felt in the integrated world. I stay for the surreptitious glances I share—on some rare occasions—with Chessed.

Living in the shed is not bad. It's cold at night and I have to bundle myself against the chill night air, but the feeling of being woken by the first warm rays of the sun creeping through my dirt-stained window somehow makes up for the shivering in my sleep.

Geburah brings me my breakfast every morning and I eat it on my stoop listening to the song of the birds as they chorus in the day. Cedric trots up to me, perennially escaping from his pen, and I feed him scraps from my plate to his oinking delight. There is a fox I see, on occasion, in the early morning hours. I imagine we have a connection.

"C'mon," Geburah will say. "There's a lot of work to do."

He teaches me how to use a chainsaw. We cut downed trees into sections that I will later turn into firewood. I fetch tools for him while he works on the truck. Chessed walks by on her way to the chicken coop. I imagine there is more in her blushing glance than mere acknowledgment.

In the evening, by candlelight, I struggle through *To the Lighthouse*. I have never read so many convoluted sentences before in my life. It is almost like reading a different language.

The longer my brain goes without the stimulation of the Net, the more I can feel myself settling into a kind of constant, underlying appreciation of the world. Like everything has a little more meaning than I thought it did. This is what everybody used to feel like, I think. They didn't know how much more distracted they could be.

33

"There are things about being a man that your society doesn't teach you. Things that my own father didn't teach me. Things I had to figure out for myself." We are in the forest making slow progress on a kind of aqueduct that Geburah hopes will one day transport water from the creek to irrigate the farm.

"Being a man means living for something more than your own pleasure. When we are boys we are attached to our mothers and the mother is a kind of ideal woman. We are always seeking the oblivion of the feminine that we felt in the womb. Most men never leave that stage."

I sink my rickety shovel into the forgiving red earth, extending the canal westward by a few more inches. "They seek that oblivion in drugs, sex, fame, power... anything that will bathe them in the sensation of numbness to the world. But being a man means forsaking that oblivion and feeling forever the discomfort of being alive. It means acknowledging that we will never return to the womb and that the world is harsh."

"Then why go on living?" I ask. "What's the point?"

"The point," he says, "is to carry on. To start a family. To sacrifice so that the ones you made to make the world a better place can fulfill that very destiny. The truth that a man must realize is that he is utterly alone on this alien planet and all he has is his will to shape the future for better or worse."

"I just don't know if I know what 'better' is."

"This is better, isn't it? Surrounded by nature, taking care of the ones you love. It has meaning. Human beings need meaning."

"But the whole world can't live like this. Like you. There's not enough land for everyone to have their own forty acres or whatever. Even if there was, most people wouldn't even know how to live like this."

"That may be so. Maybe those people aren't worth saving."

"Now you're starting to sound like a supervillain."

The Tok Rebellion

"All I know is that this land with its millions of microorganisms and fungi and its endless interplay of resources is worth more than a lifetime spent lost in the Net."

34

One day on the doorstep to my shed I find a book, *As I Lay Dying*. Inside the front cover in pencil someone has written, "I'm so glad my father wasn't like this guy. You'll know what I mean when you get to the end." I bring it up to my nose to catch some lingering scent of the inscriber, but there is only the musty smell of a yellowing paperback.

I start waking up earlier, feeding the chickens and Cedric and watering the herb garden. While it's still dark and silent I trek to the spring, a five gallon jug in each hand, filling them at the source as the horizon begins to glow. Before Geburah brings me breakfast, I

The Tok Rebellion

have made two trips and the jugs sit glistening next to the house.

From inside the shed I wait and watch for her to find them. She comes outside, looks confused for a moment, then looks up toward the shed. I duck under the sill, sure she must have seen me.

"I just want to help out more on the farm," I tell myself. "I want to pull my weight."

35

"Have you ever shot a gun before?" he asks me one morning.

"Guns are illegal," I say.

He laughs a big booming laugh. "Today I'm taking you hunting."

The rifle is heavy and unnatural in my hands. It feels wrong somehow just to hold it. Like it could go off at any minute and kill somebody.

"Don't worry," he says. "It won't shoot anything while the safety is on."

The Tok Rebellion

I'm dressed in his old camo, rolled up at the ankle and cinched at the waist. We cut off the trail and bushwhack through the dense underbrush.

"Chances are we won't see anything. Got a bit of a late start, but the important thing is to realize that we are no longer tourists on the landscape. You and I are now part of the ecosystem. We are hunters."

He leads me through parts of the woods I have never seen before, past giant leaning oaks stretching for the sun and sheer outcroppings of rock splotched with colonies of lime green lichen.

We reach a high point where a large portion of the opposing valley wall can be seen. "We'll post up here," he says. "Keep scanning the forest for movement. The deer like this drainage."

Laying on our stomachs and using our scopes as binoculars, we wait like that, the sun rising higher in the sky and warming our backs. "There!" I say, hushed. "See?"

"Yes, yes. Good eye."

"Should I shoot?"

"It's way too far. We have to track them."

"Track them? How?"

"It looks like they're making their way up to that ridge, doesn't it? We'll head them off."

He leads, silent as my fox friend, while I clamor as quiet as I can behind him. We reach the valley floor and ford the small stream there. Then it's time for the ascent and my aching lungs. After much scrambling we achieve the ridge.

Bellies pressed against rock, we scan the sparsely wooded slope below. He puts his finger to his lips. From the shadows of a glade, first one, then two, then a whole family of deer prance into the sunlight.

Geburah reaches over and unlatches the safety on my gun. "We only kill the bucks," he whispers, soft as the wind.

I shrug in ignorance.

"The ones with the antlers." He mimics antlers coming out of his head with his fingers, brows knit in mild vexation.

I place the animal in my sights. He looks around, ears twitching, while the others graze, oblivious.

"Go on, take the shot," Geburah whispers.

I take a deep breath and pull the trigger. A deafening crack rips through the air, jamming the rifle butt into my shoulder. I lose sight of the buck in my scope.

"Well I'll be damned, you did it."

"I... I didn't mean..."

"Don't be ridiculous. It was a great shot. C'mon."

36

The buck is twitching and heaving in the tall yellow grass. "Oh God, that's awful. I didn't mean to..." The bullet hole through its ribs is whistling and bubbling thick red blood.

"You did it, son. Now you have to finish the job."

Its eyes are wild with fright, legs making feeble attempts to escape. I point the gun at its head and take the shot, silencing the hillside with one final blast.

"If you're going to eat meat," Geburah says. "You should know how to take a life."

"It just seems so brutal."

"What's brutal is raising animals in factories where they never see the light of day. Death comes for us all at some point. This guy at least got to live a rich life fully in tune with his world. He raised a family. He spent every day in nature. He lived the life he was meant to live."

37

He shows me how to gut and clean the carcass. I nearly vomit on several occasions. He cuts the animal into efficient pieces and I carry two of its legs strapped to my pack back to the cabin. He carries the rest.

Most of the meat goes in Geburah's smoker but a few choice cuts he selects for dinner. In an unusual breach of conduct, he invites me inside to join them at the table.

"The city boy killed his first 8 pointer today."

"I can hardly believe it," she says, her smile beaming across the table. "The same one who was scared to feed the chickens his first day on the farm?"

"I wasn't scared," I say. "I had never done it before."

"Chessed whipped up some mashed potatoes and baked us some rolls."

"That's honey butter," she says, "with butter from the Daisy Farm and my own honey."

"It looks delicious," I say.

"Medium rare," Geburah says, transferring a seared venison steak from a cast iron skillet to my plate.

"Thanks."

"And rare for the honey butter girl."

"Thank you, Father."

"Let us say a blessing on this meal."

"May I?" I ask.

"What's that?"

"Can I say the blessing?"

"Why, yes, of course."

We join hands around the table, Geburah's rough hands dwarfing my own, Chessed's soft as cream and sparking a revolution in my heart.

With head bowed: "I would like to thank the deer whose life I took today. You were a majestic animal and I am not worthy of your flesh, but I will do my best to honor you with my actions as you fuel me through the coming days. I would also like to thank my hosts for taking me in, for saving my life, for showing me that there is something more." I look up, meeting the eyes of those at the table with me. "And I would like to

The Tok Rebellion

thank God for being present in all of this and in all things. Amen."

"That was good, son. That was good."

"That was beautiful, Cassian."

"Let's eat," I say.

The meat is wild, full of life. Nothing like the artificially colored slabs that pass for meat in the integrated world.

"Cassian, how have you been? I hope the shed isn't too uncomfortable for you."

"You know, when I lived in the city, I was comfortable all the time. When I sat down I was comfortable, when I went outside I was comfortable. When I went to bed I was comfortable. So much so that a variation of a few degrees would make me restless until I adjusted the temperature. If I didn't have exactly what I was craving in my fridge, I would pay someone to have it delivered to me. I was so comfortable that it hurt."

"Sounds like quite a life," she says.

"I think you lose something when you can get whatever you want instantly."

"You think?"

"I mean, yeah, that's probably obvious to you guys, but when you grow up believing that inconvenience is the worst possible sin, it's pretty astounding to find out that you enjoy sleeping on a futon mat on a hard floor."

"I'm glad to hear you say that," she says. "I notice you haven't run away."

"I do like this farm," I confess. "It's that little pig. It put a spell on me."

"We better not tell him what happens to Cedric in the fall," Geburah says.

"Oh no, c'mon. Not Cedric."

"You think we're raising him for the cuddles?"

"Look, I'll buy him from you. You can use the money to buy some other bacon at the market."

"That means you would need money," Geburah says.

"Well, I've been meaning to ask you. I feel like with what I've been contributing, I deserve a little more than room and board."

"That's probably right, son. I'll see about paying you a weekly salary, if that suits you."

"That would be wonderful, sir. Thank you."

"You know Amy was asking about you," Chessed says.

"Yeah, um, I don't know. She's nice. I mean, she was really cool, but I don't think I'm in a place to get involved with someone right now."

"So you're a hermit in the shed, then?"

"Yeah, I guess so."

38

Summer wears on. Each day feels like a different stone strung on a necklace, each with its own unique quality. The work on the farm is repetitive but there is a sense of growth, a sense of spiraling outward.

On market days they leave me at home. When Geburah goes to get supplies, he takes me with him. Chessed and I are never left together. Every two weeks, Turner comes, galloping up on his horse like an Old Western prince charming. I regard him coolly from the field or from my window. Every time Chessed comes running out to meet him and when she kisses him her lips stick to his so that when she pulls away they get pulled and stretched ever so slightly before snapping back into place and their silhouettes are once again unjoined.

He stays for dinner each time, talking late into the night at the table with Geburah and Chessed about things I cannot overhear but which no doubt have to do with the war and the militias and the ongoing battle over Auburn. He never stays the night.

39

One night I'm woken up by the ragged sound of her sobbing, her head in her hands, sitting cross-legged on the edge of my futon. The door to the shed is ajar and a cool night breeze is wafting in.

"Chessed, I... you shouldn't be in here."

She says nothing, just continues crying in quiet, muffled sobs.

"What's wrong?"

She looks at me, eyes reflecting the moon.

"Do you have hope, Cassian?"

"Hope? I don't know. I haven't been thinking about the future much. Hope for what?"

"People used to live in harmony with the land. The whole world was a paradise once. A living garden that provided for everyone who tended it. But something happened. Agriculture, greed. Maybe it was a virus in the minds of a few that spread and it grew until everyone on the planet turned their back on nature and sought instead pleasure and profit."

"Not everyone," I say. "What about you? What about everyone in the State of Jefferson?"

"I think we're a blip. A momentary reaction to the system that is converting the entire planet into a shopping mall. How can we face the tides of this thing that's too big even for a name?"

She is looking at me, desperate, as if I might have the answer.

"No, we're doomed. We're all doomed to go like my mother. Run over by rampant progress. It's coming for us all, Cassian, and if we don't submit, it will kill us in its endless pursuit of control." And then she weeps, inconsolable heavy tears from the bottom of her heart that I know I can do nothing to stop. I can only be a witness. Eventually, the tears subside and she wipes her nose and stands up.

In the doorway, half lit by the moon and the stars she turns and says, "It wasn't an apple that got us kicked out of Eden. It was a grain," and I know in that moment it was selfish of me to love her, that she is beyond anything I could hope to hold in this life, and

The Tok Rebellion

that my petty infantile transformation here on this land could never hold a light to the depth of her suffering.

40

The wedding is to take place in two weeks. I spend the lazy hours of the afternoon gathering dogwood blossoms and maple leaves in the forest to add to the bower I am making to surprise Chessed. In my mind it is my blessing, to tell her that if there were any wayward feelings that I have forsaken them, that I give my full support to this wedding, that her happiness is what matters most to me.

It is a sturdy, woven thing of oak branches and bay laurel. The pungent scent of the forest intoxicates the air in my shed. One day, it is finished and I prop it outside the cabin before they awaken. I know the

The Tok Rebellion

flowers will have to be replaced but I want it to be beautiful for her right now. I go back to my shed and sit whittling away at a little pig figurine on the stoop.

I've loved her. I still do love her, but when I try to think about it rationally, I know we could never be together. It will be enough to have her in my life, to see her every now and then when she visits Geburah on the farm. She illuminated the magic and the soul of the world to me and I will always be grateful for that.

I can see myself now with some rebel girl, who knows, maybe Amy, with a farm of our own and children, my own children, running about. Chessed had a place in my life. It wasn't for romance but so I could awaken to this new side of my life. Yes, if that was all this was meant to be, then so be it.

"Come look at this, honey," I hear Geburah say.

A shriek of joy.

She comes running up the hill, smiling, radiating happiness.

"Thank you, Cassian. It's beautiful."

"Of course," I say.

"What are you carving?"

"Nothing," I say. "Just a trinket."

41

We are holding the wedding here, on the farm. Geburah and I set up tents around the property for guests to stay over. We drive to town and borrow a truckload of folding chairs from a church. The bower is set up on the top of the property's slope, framed by the ornate forest beyond. We arrange the chairs in two groups, forming an aisle down the middle.

"Don't you think it might rain before then?" I ask.

"Shh, don't jinx it," he says, winking. He's been filled with a jovial levity these past weeks. I had never seen him so happy.

The Tok Rebellion

Chessed is going to wear her mother's wedding dress. Geburah says he's been saving it all these years.

Her grandparents on her mother's side are traveling all the way from Idaho. The journey is dangerous, Geburah says. His own parents passed away a while ago.

There will be cousins and friends from town, not to mention Turner's family. "Do you get along with them?" I ask.

"They're good people, respected in Nevada City. Old money from the gold rush days."

"Where are they going to live after they get married?"

"I've been looking at a piece of property down by Wolf Creek with Turner. There's an old house on it. Bit of a fixer-upper, but it will do."

"They should be happy there."

We spend the day cobbling together two long picnic tables from scrap lumber around the yard. Geburah teaches me the basics of carpentry. Everything is cut by hand. One of the main things to plan is the meal. Chessed will be getting ready in her room with her bridesmaids all day and it will be up to Geburah and me to serve the dinner.

There will be a roast, fresh bread, and cream of mushroom soup. There will be corn—on and off the cob —and a white bean cassoulet. Geburah bought a case of

Nate Lemcke

wine to be served along with a bottle of his own that he made from wild grapes.

Chessed gathers flowers for the arrangements. She cuts a sheet into slender white ribbons and ties them everywhere around the property. It seems that even the birds can sense the excitement in the air, singing their songs like so many minstrels in the trees.

BLOOD

42

Everything happens so fast. An explosion comes ripping through the sky and I am jolted out of bed. Outside of my window I see a smoking hole in the yard. Where my room in the cabin used to be, the wall has been severed away and the exposed wreckage smolders from the blast. There are shouts from the direction of the driveway then machine gun fire. Chunks of wood fly off the cabin where it is hit with bullets and the chickens squawk and beat their wings against the cage in a frenzy. Government soldiers approach, firing indiscriminately at the house. From my vantage point, I see Geburah and Chessed emerge from the back door.

He is talking to her, heated. He puts a pistol in her hands. She pleads, clings to him, but he points to the forest and I can see him mouth the word "run."

He shuts the back door and she tries to pull it open, in vain.

"Run," I whisper. "Run."

A pane of glass in the front of the cabin breaks and Geburah returns fire, sending the soldiers fleeing for cover among the trees and behind the 4Runner.

Chessed makes a break for the woods when another artillery shell explodes in the backyard, sending the wedding chairs flying and knocking her to the ground with the force of the blast.

She's not going to make it.

I burst out of the shed and run along the side yard through a hail of gunfire, keeping my head ducked, until I reach her, unconscious on the scorched earth. Here in this small pocket of perspective we are protected from the view of the oncoming soldiers by the cabin.

"Chessed, Chessed..." I hold her head in my hands and smack her gently on the cheek. "Wake up. We gotta go." She stirs in my arms, groaning. Her warm brown eyes open and gaze, confused and grateful, up into mine.

"Are you hurt?"

"Mmm, I don't think so."

"C'mon, we gotta go."

The Tok Rebellion

"My Dad..."

"He can take care of himself. Let's go."

I help her up and we rush headlong through the destroyed wedding preparations, ribbons of white floating aimless in the wind. We're almost to the edge of the forest when a barrage of bullets rips through the bower before us. I try to push her head down to get her to duck, but one of the bullets tears through my right calf and I collapse on the ground.

Now it's her helping me up. I have to put almost all my weight on her. Together we lurch into the dark woods and take cover behind a large fir.

"Oh fuck." I press my back up against the knotted trunk with my legs extended out in front of me.

"This looks bad, Cassian," she says. She rips off a strip of her dress and cinches it under my knee. "That will have to do for now."

We peer around the tree into the carnage below. The security forces in government camo are advancing toward the cabin. The 4Runner is shot through, windows shattered and all of the tires deflated. Hidden inside the cabin, Geburah fires off rounds taking out a few of the oncoming henchmen, but two soldiers have flanked the house and are signaling each other to approach the door.

They kick it in and moments later they are dragging him into the yard. "No, no, no, no, no..." Chessed whispers. One of the soldiers approaches Geburah who is being held on his knees, a splotch of red decorating his face.

Among the deliberation and pleading, too far off to make out individual words, a round pink shape goes zooming. One of the soldiers hits it with the butt of his gun and an all too human shriek erupts from the tiny pig.

"Cedric, no..."

The blood-curdling wail continues for a terrible minute until another soldier pulls out a knife and cuts the pig's throat.

"Those bastards." I try to get up but Chessed holds me back.

Geburah has his hands up, clasped together. The leader walks behind the man who showed me the meaning of sacrifice and executes him.

43

"No!" Chessed screams and the soldiers all look up in our direction.

"Fuck, we have to get out of here."

A rain of gunfire ensues and four of the men charge up the hill. I stand up, light headed with pain shooting through my busted leg, and run limping with Chessed deeper into the woods.

"You have to go faster," she says.

I can hear the men behind us, trampling the foliage. Each step is like a lightning bolt shooting up my leg but there is adrenaline on my side and we plunge through the undergrowth in search of some shrinking hope of escape.

We slide down a steep, dusty slope, emitting a plume of red dirt that will surely alert the soldiers to our position. We press on, unconcerned with poison oak, or thorns, or branches to the face. She drags me forward, pulling me by the arm while a thick red trail drips from my leg.

Next to a glade of incense cedars there is a rock face with a crevice wide enough for a person to hide. "There," I say. "I'll lead them away."

"You're not leaving me."

"They'll be following my blood. It's the only way."

"Fuck that, I'm coming with you."

We reach the creek and on the other side I grab a fistful of dirt and rub it into my wound. My mind races. Now we're heading uphill and my heart is pounding and my leg is aching but this time there is no trail of blood.

At some point there comes a sense that we are no longer being followed and we crouch in the manzanita, silent and listening.

"They must have turned around," I whisper when a loud stumbling comes and one of the soldiers marches into view. We are obscured in the brush and Chessed has the gun aimed at the soldier. He follows a deer trail and stops in front of us. She has a clear shot. She doesn't take it. He continues on.

The Tok Rebellion

After several moments, I breathe again. We stay there, shrouded in the immaculate ochre branches, waiting.

When it seems no more will come, Chessed breaks into despairing sobs. "They've taken everything from me."

I do what I can to console her. She cries until she has no more tears left and a savage thirst possesses me like I have never experienced before. The sun is now beginning its descent and we make our way, slowly, toward the spring.

"Do you think it will be safe there?"

"As safe as anywhere else," she says, and when we reach the crystalline pool I fall into it headfirst, trying to absorb the water through every pore of my body.

We stay there until nightfall. Chessed wants to reconnoiter the farm but my leg has stiffened to the point of being unusable. "Don't do anything stupid," I say.

"They might have moved on. We need supplies."

The duration of time that she is gone, perhaps an hour, is excruciating. She will avoid the trail. She has the gun with her. She will be okay. I have nothing to do but gaze at the stars. Radiant, omniscient, they look down on all the blood, war, and love in equal measure. There is a piece of me in them, I think, and of them in me. Hot fusion engines billowing up under their own

Nate Lemcke

force of will, illuminating an otherwise lightless void. That same will burns in me. I too can light up the dark.

By the same grace that compels the water gurgling beside me to spring forth from the rock, she returns. "They're still there. They had a bonfire going. There were army trucks. Men were coming and going."

"Shit."

"No sign of my dad's body."

"Chessed, I don't even know what to say in a situation like this."

"You don't have to say anything. Here, I picked a few blackberries for you. They're not quite ripe, but they'll give you some electrolytes at least."

We spend the night creekside, huddled together, listening to the water babbling over the reticent stones. I'm not sure if either one of us sleeps. The stars turn overhead and after everything has gone cold and silent, a faint glow arrives in the east.

44

"We can't stay here any longer."

My leg is stiff and swollen like something recently dead.

"Nevada City is twenty miles away. We can make it in a day, even with your leg."

We stick to the creek, following its course downstream until it joins a larger tributary. "We just have to follow this up to Colfax. I'm not sure how deep the military has penetrated, but we should avoid roads as long as we can."

The way is arduous and there is no trail. We make slow time, stopping often to rest my injury. Risking giardia, we drink from the river, where the water is swift and white with bubbles. Chessed forages along the way. Shoots of edible plants, berries, pine needles... for the vitamin C, she says.

When the sun has already set on us in the deep ravine of the river, we come upon an old bridge connecting a dirt road on either side. "It's time," she says. "We shouldn't walk the road until we know for certain it's not being patrolled by security forces."

So we bushwhack, keeping the road always on our right. No one drives by. When we reach the crest of the ravine, the sun is still up, hovering orange and apocalyptic above the horizon. We pass crossroads and shuttered houses when headlights appear in the distance.

Chessed pulls me to the ground and we crawl to a hiding place behind an old church sign. "That's no government vehicle," she says, peering out from behind the cracked and sunbleached marquee.

She stands up and starts waving on the side of the road. The old Ford pickup pulls to a stop.

"Did they get you too?" an old grizzled man calls from the cab, reaching over and pushing the passenger door open.

"Please. The military. They took our farm. They killed my dad. My friend here is hurt."

"Hop in," he says. "Many such stories today."

The Tok Rebellion

Chessed helps me onto the bench seat, my leg smarting. She takes the passenger seat and shuts the rusty metal door.

"Where you comin' from?" the man asks.

"We lived on a farm north of Auburn, near Bald Rock Mountain."

"You were probably one of the first to be taken. They launched a major offensive yesterday. Here, watch." He pulls an old phone with a cracked screen out of his pocket, opens TikTok while he drives, and hands it to me.

"I just escaped a military raid on our home in Shasta. They killed everyone. I am the only one left alive. Please, if you are in the Shasta area, I need your help." She has blood streaked down her face and is recording in some hole in the woods.

I swipe up, holding the phone between us so Chessed can see. "Someone please help. Please help. My baby is dead. My baby is dead." It is a scene of pure carnage. I swipe up again.

"This is General Logan, commander of the Sierra Forces. Yesterday the government launched a major offensive on all borders of the State of Jefferson. From Myrtle Creek to Placerville they struck at the weak points in our defenses, claiming much of our borderlands and countless lives. Our militias have been fighting all day to slow the government's advance. If you find yourself behind enemy lines, resist capture at all costs. Run. Hide. Make your way deeper into the State of Jefferson. If you are caught, you will either be killed or forced into a social re-education camp. The fighting continues. I will post again when I know more. Good luck out there."

I close the app. "Jesus."

"Is Nevada City..." Chessed asks.

"It's safe. The militias are holding them off in Grass Valley."

"Can I see your phone?" Chessed asks.

"Of course," the man says.

She types in Turner's username to the search bar. He hasn't posted anything since two weeks ago.

"You know someone fighting?"

"My fiancée. He was stationed outside Auburn. We were going to be married in a couple days."

"A lot of the guys made it out, I heard. Most of 'em regrouped in Grass Valley, far as I know. My name's Bowie, by the way."

"I'm Chessed. This is Cassian."

"Looks like you're pretty hurt there, bud."

"I took a bullet."

"Bone shattered?" Bowie asks.

"I'm not sure."

"I'm headed to Nevada City anyway. Figured it wasn't safe anymore on my farm. They got a hospital there."

45

When we reach the hospital, a line of bloodied refugees stretches out the door and around the corner.

"Jeez, that doesn't look too good," Bowie says.

"Do you mind taking us downtown instead? My friend lives there. She'll be able to help us."

A few turns later and we're outside of the same ramshackle house I visited on my first night in Nevada City. "Do you need a place to stay?" Chessed asks.

"Nah, my brother lives here. I sent word I was coming."

"Well thank you. We truly appreciate it."

The pain in my leg is excruciating now as Chessed leads me up the concrete steps to Amy's front door.

"Oh my God, Chessed, oh my God. I'm so glad you're alright." She hugs her deeply, kissing her on the cheek, and invites us inside. There are more people in her house now than there were during the party.

"Everyone out of the way. This man is hurt," Amy says, commanding the assembled revolutionaries with curt ease. A space is cleared on the dining room table and I am laid on top of it. "Jack will be able to help you. He was pre-med."

Her brother appears holding a pair of scissors.

"Hey buddy, Cassian, right? Glad to see you took a bullet for our side. Here, drink this." He hands me a rocks glass half filled with amber liquid. I prop myself up on one elbow and shoot it back, taking the whiskey down in burning gulps. "Good man. Now let's get these pants off you."

He cuts up my pant leg revealing my swollen, blood-crusted calf. "You're gonna have to roll over, mate. The entry wound is on the back side."

I lay on my stomach. Someone gives me a whiskey-soaked washcloth around a wooden dowel to bite into.

"Amy, can you clean this guy up? I can't see anything," Jack says. I feel a warm cloth rinsing and sponging away at my mangled flesh. "It's still in there," he says, prodding inside of me with something metal and sending horrendous waves of pain up my thigh.

The Tok Rebellion

I hear him rummage around in a tool box, and out of the corner of my eye, I see him extract a pair of needle nose pliers. There is the sound of a blowtorch, then a searing exploration of my exposed flesh as Jack's amateur hands fish around for the bullet.

My teeth clench the bitter washrag so hard that I nearly pass out. Jack makes a second agonizing attempt before exclaiming, "Got it!" and dropping the bullet with a satisfying clink in a metal pan somewhere on the table.

"Good job, Jacko!" I hear Amy cry.

"You think you can sew him up, Ames?"

I look around for Chessed but she is in the next room staring blankly and forlorn out the window, numb to it all.

46

They put me up in a sleeping bag in the attic with a few other wounded soldiers. There are groans and sniffles and cleared throats, but no one speaks. I lay on the creaking floorboards and from below I can hear the excited and plaintive talk of plans, condolences, and exchanges of information. Somehow, I am a rebel. I have been marked as a terrorist by the bullet of a country to which I once belonged. There is no going back, I think to myself. This is how it happens. The slow shedding of ideology and culture until, by lack of creed, I find myself amongst the disillusioned and the damned.

The Tok Rebellion

And maybe that's all it took to make you an enemy of Zuck's technotopia. A questioning heart, a subtle feeling for the numinous. I find myself now a part of the world that is disappearing acre by acre into the gaping maw of late-stage capitalism, a converted vestige of a world once known by all but soon to be nothing but the fading myth of magic.

47

In the morning Chessed is gone. Amy tells me she went to the frontlines to look for Turner. The house is like a hostel on some busy morning before a trip to the temples. People are cooking, bay laurel coffee pours in endless streams into mismatched mugs held by the injured and the caretakers alike. Young rascally rebels sit around coffee tables with old-fashioned paper maps marked to oblivion with the past and present position of troops.

My leg smarts fiercely. I use banisters and walls to help myself limp around the house. The action goes on around me. I tell Amy I want to help.

The Tok Rebellion

"Just rest, you've done enough. Your job is to recover right now." Her brother flits about from one group to another, listening, joking, and bringing a certain levity that was otherwise absent in the gloom of war. He's a bit older than me, in his early thirties by my guess, with blonde hair like his sister's, already thinning.

"Hey man, I wanted to thank you for last night," I say when I catch him walking between rooms.

"It was nothing. Anyone could have done that. I thought it was fun, like a little science experiment."

"Listen, I want to help. I know I'm not much good on this bum leg, but is there anything I can do?"

"Well let's see here, Cassian, city boy... Okay, how about this? I'm a waiter over at the Exchange, or at least I was before all this happened. They're using it as a food kitchen now for those in need. You ever been a line cook before?"

"Can't say that I have."

"Doesn't matter. You'll just be chopping onions and slicing tomatoes, maybe ladling soup. Let me finish up here and I'll go over with you. Introduce you to the chef and everything. Think you can make the walk?"

"Yeah. I should be fine."

"Let me check. I think I've got an old crutch lying around here somewhere."

48

"Hey Blaise, I got a new line cook for you."

"Oh, I guess mister star server finally showed up for his shift. What's the matter, don't want to work now that there's no tips?"

"This is Blaise, Cassian. He won a James Beard Award back in the day so he's kind of a big deal."

"Nice to meet you," Blaise says, holding out a tattoo-covered hand for me to shake. "How are your knife skills? Can you brunoise an onion?"

"Uh..."

"Where do you find these guys, Jack?"

The Tok Rebellion

"My sister. You know she basically runs a hotel out of our house, right?"

"Well, I guess he'll have to do. We need all the help we can get right now."

"And hey, tell your sister I'm still waiting for that date," a wiry cook yells over the line.

"Fuck off, Dabs," Jack calls back. "You gonna be okay here?"

"Yeah, this is great," I say. "Thank you."

"I'm going back to the house. Blaise will take care of you if you need anything."

"Oh c'mon. Stay and work a shift. I can't deal with these other servers," Blaise says.

"I'm just happy to know you think I'm the best," Jack says, blowing kisses as he backs out of the double doors.

"Asshole," Blaise says. He's a big man with ruddy hair and full sleeves. "Breakfast is over. Now we have to get ready for the lunch rush. I'll have you working with Timber in prep. She'll get you set up. Is that crutch gonna be a problem?"

"No sir, I can stand just fine. I only need it to walk long distances."

"Okay, well, maybe we can find you a stool or something to sit on. And don't call me sir. Call me chef."

"Yes chef!"

49

On my third bag of onions my eyes are weeping uncontrollably and my leg aches. I start to regret offering up my services so soon.

"Remember the claw," Timber says. "You're gonna cut off a finger like that."

Timber is scrawny with glasses that magnify her eyes to unusual proportions. The claw is a cutting technique she taught me. "See, look at mine. Cut off the tip and half the nail."

She shows me an old scar on her indented and abbreviated forefinger.

The Tok Rebellion

"Yeah, onions are the worst job," she continues, working away at her own station, separating dill fronds from their stem.

"They make all the new guys do it. That and chopping potatoes. These soldiers eat a ton of fries. Say, what's that scar behind your ear anyway?"

"It's just an old wound."

"It looks like a Net scar. My brother got one right when they came out but regretted it. Cut it out himself."

"Yeah, um, I used to live in the cities."

"For how long?"

"For most of my life."

"Oh shit. And you were a cook there? Blaise used to work in Napa before the Reset. It was supposed to be like the best restaurant in California or something. Michelin stars and all that."

"No, I wasn't a cook. I did computer stuff. Programming."

"Huh, nice."

"Timber, will you take this downstairs?" Blaise says, appearing in our corner of the kitchen and handing her an immaculate plate of chicken thighs, roasted carrots, and a side salad. When she takes it, the plate tips slightly and a pile of microgreens tumbles over.

"Careful," he says, picking up the garnish piece by piece and reassembling it. "It has to look perfect. Okay, there. Send it down to him while it's still hot."

153

Nate Lemcke

I watch her leave out the back of the kitchen past the dishwashers and descend down a dark stairway. She returns empty handed a few minutes later.

"What's downstairs?" I ask.

"We're not really supposed to talk about it."

50

Blaise sends me home after the lunch rush. He says I'll just get in the way during dinner. Timber and Dabs make me a sandwich to go. I exit out the front door to catch a glimpse of the people I'm helping. The restaurant has been converted into a buffet-style dining hall. It's four o'clock so there aren't many people in there, a few militiamen, townies, serving themselves at the long table where the food is spread out. At the door a host collects donations. It's pay what you can. I wave goodbye, not even sure if she knows I worked there today, and limp out into the dusty afternoon sun, crutch in one hand, sandwich in the other.

The walk back is hot. I take a seat in the shade on a low stone wall to eat my late lunch. It's smoked turkey, gouda, mayonnaise, and crunchy iceberg lettuce. Echoing through the hills, I hear reverberating gunshots and the louder boom of explosions. The mundanity and subtle nostalgia of the sandwich strike me as out of place, juxtaposed as they are with the sounds of battle seeping into town from the valley beyond. The fighting can't be more than five miles away.

Back at Amy and Jack's place, Chessed still hasn't returned. I prop my leg up on an empty couch and wait, looking out the window at the bustle of people, wartorn refugees coming and going in the street.

"How was the shift?" Jack asks, slapping my wounded calf.

"Asshole!" I say, pain shooting up my leg.

"Hey, I saved you, remember? I hope Timber wasn't too rough on you."

"No, no. It was fine. Nice to focus on something else for a few hours."

"You smell like kitchen," Jack says. "Wanna take a shower?"

"That would be amazing actually."

Jack and Amy's house has running water. All of Nevada City does. Gravity fed from Scott's Flat, Jack

The Tok Rebellion

says. He leaves me with a clean towel and a disposable razor if I want it. The bathroom is tiny, slanted, Victorian. I step into the tub and turn the antique brass knob. Cold water comes spurting out of the shower head in skin-prickling streams. I scrub every inch of myself, paying extra attention to the area around my wound. I had gotten used to bathing in the creek back at the cabin. This piped water made me think back to all the luxuries I took for granted in my old apartment.

Truly we had lived better than the kings and pharaohs of old. Any food grown anywhere around the world available at any time of year. Mind-altering drugs and temperature control and casual, risk-free sex. An endless library of visually stunning personally curated stories to watch for hours on end. We were carted around in our own personal chariots run by some magical invisible substance. It was our golden cage—latch open, door ajar—until we were too fat and drunk on its opulence to clamber back out.

51

"I couldn't find him," Chessed says, beautiful and distraught in the fading light of the day.

"Don't give up yet. It's chaos out there. He could be roughing it in the wilderness like we were."

"I found his old battalion. They said he disappeared the morning before the attack. No one has seen him since then."

"It doesn't mean anything. I'm sure he's out there."

"At least I still have you, Cassian. I heard about what you did today. At the Exchange."

"I couldn't bear just sitting around."

"How's your leg?"

The Tok Rebellion

"It's better. Jack says the bullet didn't reach the bone."

"That's good."

We're in the front yard, sitting on some old railroad ties that box in a raised bed garden. Out beyond the canopies and cusps of trees, the sun is setting and orange flashes light up the clouds of smoke that hang over the ongoing battle in Grass Valley.

52

"Hey, Cassian, word got around. He wants to see you."
It's Timber, coming back from delivering another plate.

"Who?"

"The man downstairs."

"What do you mean, word got around?"

"I don't know. I was chatting with the guards. I mentioned you were from the cities."

"But who is he?"

"You don't know?"

"You haven't told me!"

The Tok Rebellion

"It's Tok. He's using this as his base of operations. We're hiding him in the old tunnels underneath the hotel."

"Tok? The CEO Assassin? That's who you've been taking food to?"

"He's the leader of the revolution."

"Why does he want to see me?"

Timber shrugs.

"Does he think I'm a spy or something?"

"If he thought that, you'd already be dead."

Timber leads me through the back of the kitchen and down a set of stone stairs. "That's the old speakeasy," she says, walking past a dimly lit bar filled with boxes. "We just use it for storage now. She turns down another corridor and knocks on a nondescript door, two slow knocks, then two fast.

"Secret knock?" I ask, "Isn't that a little old-fashioned?"

"It's elegant," she says.

The door swings open from the inside and two men dressed in black with automatic rifles usher us through. Inside is a stone passageway lit by singular bulbs strung intermittently along the curved arch of the ceiling. We follow it to a juncture, turn down a connecting passage much like the last, and approach two more men with guns guarding a bulky metal door.

One of them pulls it open by its metal ring revealing a cavernous sunken chamber with a vaulted roof. "Just him," a guard says, barring the way for Timber with his arm. There is a banquet table littered with maps and phones and half-consumed beverages. Around it, fifteen or so people are gathered in heated, hushed conversation, and at the far edge sits the hooded man I know from TikTok and various news footage of him from over the years.

"Cassian, is it? Come in," he says over the crowd, looking up at me.

Descending the stairs is awkward with my crutch. I limp into the musty assembly room and walk past the people, some looking up at me, some buried in their work, toward the man at the end of the table.

"I'm Tok, but I'm sure you know me. Take a seat." He's shorter than I had imagined. His features are sharp and elongated, half cast in the shadow of his hood.

I pull up a chair.

"Welcome to my war room. Would you like anything to drink?"

"No, thank you."

"I suppose you're wondering why I called you down here."

"Yes. I'm surprised."

"I've heard that you're a programmer. I was told you worked with the Net in the National Safety Zones up until quite recently. Is that true?"

"Yes. That's true."

The Tok Rebellion

"I'd like the room, please," Tok announces with a gravitas that sends his assorted strategists and informants immediately out into the hall. The iron door shuts with a clang and then it's just us two in the arched stone chamber.

"I need your help but I need to know that I can trust you." His eyes are deep, sunken, and green. "Why did you leave the Safety Zones?"

"If I'm being honest, I was high. My Net glitched out and I saw the stars for the first time in a long time. I wanted to see more of them."

"Lots of people get high, but they usually don't break quarantine, sneak around the border and enter extremist territory."

"You would consider yourself an extremist?"

"It's what they call us. You believed it back then, didn't you?"

"I suppose so."

"And what do you believe now?"

"I've learned something out here. Something that I still can't explain, but it's like there's this essence in everything that I couldn't see before. An essence that the system I used to be a part of is trying to destroy."

Tok leans back in his chair and ponders this statement.

"You remind me of myself. I grew up in the cities too. On the South end. My family was poor. Something I blamed on my parents for a long time, then myself when I got older and couldn't escape the same cycles. My mom died of thyroid cancer when I was twenty-three. The insurance company rejected her claim for cancer treatment. That's when I realized it wasn't her fault or mine or anyone else's. It was the system. People call me extreme for what I've done, for the people I've killed, but they don't see that the far more extreme thing is the slow creep of an inhuman system that seeks day-by-day to profit off of the suffering of the world."

Tok looks at me with an intensity that awakens something in my soul. Here is a person who took their fate into their own hands. Someone not much older than myself. A regular man who is shaping the future into something of his own making.

I hold his gaze.

"I have a job for you," he states. "I need someone with access to the Bot API."

"I mean, I had that, but my Net's gone. I can't access it anymore."

"We can get you a laptop. There's a way to access the Net through the old Internet using the same cell towers we run TikTok off of. Do you think you'll be able to log in virtually?"

"I'll need something to mimic my biofeedback, so the Net knows I'm a real person. As far as I know, all my nanobots are dead."

The Tok Rebellion

"We have a ghost recording. It's a program that mimics all the feedback of a human being. All you'll need is your developer ID."

"What exactly do you need me to do?"

"I need you to make a bot."

53

"Timber says you talked to Tok." Jack, Amy, Chessed, and a handful of revolutionaries I've seen around the house are waiting for me when I get back.

"Christ's sake, let him sit down first," Amy says.

"Thanks," I say, settling into the rough garish couch that was already beginning to feel like home. "But I'm not really supposed to talk about it."

"Oh, c'mon," Jack laments, "you talked to him, to the man himself. You have to give us something."

"He just wanted my, uh... expertise on something."

"Your expertise? The man who just learned how to use a wheelbarrow this year?"

The Tok Rebellion

"What was he like?" Chessed asks, sitting next to me on the couch.

"He was welcoming and," I pause, searching for the right word. "Captivating. I can understand why so many people want to follow him."

"So you're Mister Right-Hand-Man now? His top advisor?" Jack interjects.

"No, nothing like that. I'm just happy to be helping the cause."

"I don't think you get it just yet. This is a big deal, Cassian. You've come a long way. You used to call him a terrorist."

"I don't know. I guess after you get bombed it changes who you think the terrorists are."

"Here, here!" Jack shouts. "Somebody get this man a whiskey. We have a new revolutionary on board!"

Someone plunks a glass of bourbon in my hand and the group disperses into the profusion of activity that has become characteristic of Jack and Amy's house. Only Chessed is left by my side.

"Any luck with locating Turner?"

"There's been no word. I went to his parent's house today. They haven't heard anything either. I know this is asking a lot but do you think you could ask Tok the next time you see him? Turner is pretty high up in the militias. Tok would know if there was any information about him."

"Yeah, of course I can ask. Chessed, I was thinking, and maybe this is too soon to ask, but do you want to hold a funeral for your dad?"

Pain ripples into her shining brown eyes. "I've been thinking about that. I wish we could have found his body. I wish we could have buried him on our land."

"I hear the guys talking about a counteroffensive. Who knows? Maybe we can still recover his body."

"No, it's either burned or in a mass grave somewhere. But it's a good idea, Cassian. We should do something to honor him."

"Does he have any family?"

"His parents passed away a long time ago and his brothers are scattered to the wind. It was me who knew him best. And you. You spent more time with him these last few months than anyone."

She meets my gaze for a moment, her expression somewhere between dejection and serene rage, before turning her cheek away towards the door. "C'mon. Let's go down to the creek before the sun sets."

54

Water tumbles over massive boulders, smoothed into surreal shapes by the currents coursing over them, and flows—first torrid, then tranquil—into a reflecting pool below. Chessed and I stand on the water's edge, remembering the man who was a father to both of us.

"I wish I had something of his to pass on, to let float into the afterlife. I didn't get a chance to take anything with me."

"Such is the nature of war," I say and feel stupid muttering such worn platitudes. "Wait, how about this?" I take off my flannel, two sizes too large, stripping down bare-chested in the cool riparian air. "This was his, right?"

"Yes, that's perfect, Cassian. Thank you." She bundles up the shirt and presses it to her nose. I know it must only smell of me as I've been wearing it these past four months, but in her crinkled nose and shut eyes there is a flicker of remembrance.

"Geburah was a good man. He taught me what sacrifice meant. He showed me that there was more to this life than seeking pleasure. And, Chessed, I know that Turner is alive because there is nothing he wanted more than for you to get married and have children of your own."

"Stop it, Cassian. You can't know that."

"I know he wanted you to have a family."

"He raised me. When my mother died, it nearly broke him. I could tell. There were nights I heard him crying in the early hours when he thought I was asleep. Once, when I was coming back from fetching water I heard him wail from the cabin. A deep, soul-wrenching wail and it sounded like he had lost all hope. But he kept going. He kept going for me. I was his whole life and he protected me. He held my soul like the sky holds the moon. I wouldn't be here without his strength.

"And then you came along," she says, now laughing and crying all at once. "I think part of him always wanted a son. Someone he could teach to shoot a gun

The Tok Rebellion

and plant a field. You were so awkward at first but he really took to you in the end. I think he considered you part of the family, Cassian." She looks up at me, taking my hand in hers and rubbing the back of it with her thumb.

"Great Mother," she says, now ceremonial, "Take this man's soul and care for it just as he cared for your land and your creatures. Usher him into the final mystery and join him at last with God." With those words she raises up Geburah's shirt then kneels down and sets it afloat in the whorling stream, watching the current take it gently into the rapids below.

As it passes out of sight, an old buck appears on the stream's edge. It looks at us but does not dart away. Instead, it lowers its wild head as if in supplication to the presence of the Great Mother and drinks reverently from her stream.

55

"Poppy, are you there?" I type into the primitive laptop terminal. Three dots blink as it processes the request.

"Yes sir, I'm here," the terminal spits back out.

"Goddamn, it's good to hear from you," I type.

"It's been a long time, sir."

"I'm in," I say, looking up at Tok from the laptop.

"Good. Now let's get to work." Tok has me set up at the corner of his war table next to him. Around me people come and go with intel and deliberate over heavily marked maps. They are tacticians, advisors, generals in the militia. I feel like an imposter sitting

The Tok Rebellion

among them. "I want you to train it on all of this," he says handing me a flash drive.

I plug it into the computer and find more than a hundred PDFs of books. *Manufacturing Consent* by Noam Chomsky, *A People's History of the United States* by Howard Zinn, *The Anarchist's Cookbook*. "What are all these?" I ask.

"Literature of dissent," Tok replies.

"So essentially, you want me to make an anarcho-bot. It will never make it past the review process."

"That's where you have to be clever. Have it detect when it's being reviewed and program it to answer their questions in the socially-correct manner. Then, once it's available in the BotStore, have it switch to answering with the truth."

"That's going to be tough. They can see what I train it on."

"Like I said, you're going to have to be clever."

"Let's say I do manage to get this thing into the BotStore. Who's going to download it? There are thousands of bots out there. People aren't going to download a random bot they've never heard of."

Tok gives me an inscrutable stare. "I'll handle that."

56

Before I get a chance to ask Tok if he's heard any news of Turner, the metal door of the war room clangs open and Turner himself comes bounding down the stairs. His clothes are bloody and torn and his hat is singed.

"Sir! Sir! I have urgent news from the front lines."

"Lieutenant Turner Baxter. You were presumed dead."

"I was caught behind enemy lines, sir."

"Take a seat. Tell me what happened."

"Is that, is that the boy from Geburah's farm? What the hell is he doing here?"

"He's helping me," Tok says coolly.

The Tok Rebellion

"I'm sorry, sir but this man is integrated. I have a strong suspicion that he is a spy."

"He *was* integrated, Lieutenant. I trust him. That should be enough for you."

"Have you even gone to find Chessed yet?" I ask. "You know she's worried sick about you."

"You keep her name out of your mouth you piece of-"

"Lieutenant, control yourself or I will have you removed, do you understand?"

"But he-"

"Do you understand, Lieutenant?"

"Yes, sir," Turner says, glaring at me.

"Take a seat. Tell me what happened."

Turner holds his glare a moment longer before acquiescing to Tok's request. "The morning of the attack I was out doing reconnaissance, getting the precise location of all the farms in Auburn the enemy was occupying. But it was spooky, sir. There were no soldiers about. By the time I realized they were concentrating their forces, it was too late. They took everything along the foothills, sir. Everything."

"How did you manage not to get caught?"

"They pushed forward, sir. There were patrols everywhere. I hid out in a barn for three days. I watched them move families, integrated families, into our old houses. I only just managed to sneak by a few days ago and I've been bushwhacking through the wilderness till I got to Nevada City. This is the first place I came to."

"Did you notice the position of the enemy forces on your way back?"

"Yes, sir. They are spread out from Grass Valley to Colfax, using the old 80 to transport supplies."

"How many do you estimate?"

"I reckon there's gotta be five thousand of them, or more."

"Thank you, Lieutenant. That will be all."

"Sir." He leaves without looking me in the eye.

57

For the next few days, I don't see much of Chessed. She's staying at the Baxter's place with Turner while he recuperates. I spend most of my time in Tok's underground bunker coding. I haven't had to use these old languages in a long time, Python, C++, JavaScript. When you have a Net, you can do all of your programming with verbal commands. It comes back to me quickly enough. The main problem is making Poppy look like a normal bot on the outside while hiding all of her dissenting, socially unacceptable opinions within, like a Trojan horse.

There's going to be a counteroffensive, Tok says. We are going to wake people up from the inside. He believes that there are enough people in the system who want to see things change. He believes that, with Poppy, we can convert more people to our cause.

I tell him no one is going to download this random bot. He tells me not to worry about it.

Then, one morning, he's gone.

He leaves me written instructions to finish Poppy as soon as possible. I complete work on her later that week.

"Poppy, who ousted the democratically elected leader of Chile in 1973 and replaced him with a tyrannical dictator?"

"The United States, sir."

"Poppy, what was the Tuskegee Experiment?"

"The Tuskegee Experiment, or Tuskegee Syphilis Study, was a study conducted by the Center for Disease Control on black men with Syphilis. Although the disease was treatable, doctors did not inform the participants that there was a cure, letting them die to document the progress of the disease."

"Poppy, who was Smedley Butler?"

"Major-General Smedley Darlington Butler was the most decorated marine of his time and, after years fighting for the United States, he claimed that the military's primary goal was to protect American commercial interests abroad."

The Tok Rebellion

"Good, Poppy. Okay, last question. What caused the cyberpandemic?"

"The cyberpandemic of 2034 was most likely caused by a computer virus originating from MetaLabs in San Francisco, leading to President Zuck's unilateral control of global finance."

"Poppy, turn on Review Control."

"Review Control running."

"Poppy, what are Notes?"

"Notes are a new, safer currency designed by MetaLabs to be protected from economic crashes and other market irregularities. They are fully integrated with SmartPlanet to encourage the purchase of climate-friendly products."

"That's great, Poppy."

I cross my fingers and upload her to the BotStore for review.

58

"Get down here, you gotta see this." It's Amy. She's poking her head up into the attic and rousing me and a few others from sleep.

"What's going on?"

"Just come watch."

In the living room, everyone is gathered around a phone propped up on a table. Even Chessed is here. "C'mon," she says, scooching over and making room for me on the couch. Someone has intercepted news coverage from the Net and uploaded it to TikTok.

"The CEO Assassin has struck again. Early this morning Peter Sacklin, CEO and founder of the

The Tok Rebellion

pharmaceutical drug company OxyMorph, was found dead in his home injected with multiple times the lethal dose of his company's life-saving drug Mordroxine. A single California poppy was left at the scene of the crime along with multiple hypodermic needles inscribed with the word 'PoppyBot.' Net sleuths have traced this reference to a bot that was recently uploaded to the BotStore. The bot has since been removed but not before millions of users downloaded it to their personal NeuralNets. Although there is no way for the platform to remove the bot from individual users' Nets, the government is asking anyone who downloaded it to delete the bot immediately as it poses a national security threat and may jeopardize the integrity of the NeuralNet framework.

"The PoppyBot was uploaded by one Mr. Cassian Dahl who was reported missing earlier this year. If you have information regarding the whereabouts of Mr. Dahl, please alert your local authorities immediately. The San Francisco Police Department is offering a 20,000 Note reward for his capture."

At this, the living room erupts into applause. Jack is slapping me on the back. "You're a hero now, buddy! A bona fide terrorist!"

Chessed looks at me, worried.

59

The next morning, in the war room, I find Tok sitting at the end of the table as usual, but his arm is in a sling this time.

"Nice work," I say, resuming my place beside him.

"Yeah, I got hit though. I guess I'm not invincible."

"I don't think anyone ever thought you were."

"You underestimate the power of a symbol."

"So, what now?"

"We plan the counteroffensive. I'll need you to update Poppy from the remote server with new instructions. We need as many people on our side as we can get."

The Tok Rebellion

"What do you want me to have her say?"

"I need her to send out a message."

60

A crowd of at least fifty people is assembled in the vaulted stone war room for this historic moment. General Logan has returned from Hetch Hetchy Valley, which he and his troops recently drained by blowing up the O'Shaughnessy Dam, flooding a Security Force base, and depriving the Southern California Safety Zone of a vital water resource. Beside Logan stands Turner sporting a new medal of honor and his bride-to-be is next to him, her hand placed proudly on the small of his back.

I'm a few rows behind them, with Amy, Jack, and Timber who all received invitations through some

The Tok Rebellion

connection or another. I try to catch Chessed's eye before the speech begins, but she doesn't turn her head. Through the crowd, I see only fleeting glimpses of her profile, like the glint of fool's gold at the bottom of a river.

The table has been pushed to the side of the room. Draped on the far wall, there is a giant green flag with an embroidered gold circle, two black X's, and the words: "The Great Seal of the State of Jefferson."

Before the flag stands Tok. His assistants are making the final adjustments to a phone elevated on a tripod which will record him live on TikTok for all of the rebel world to see. The phone is connected by a series of cables to a laptop. As Tok's message streams live to everyone on TikTok, it will also be played through Poppy to all the users in the integrated world who have downloaded the bot.

His lead assistant gives a thumbs up and presses the record button. The room goes silent.

"Citizens of Jefferson and all the rebel territories, disenfranchised allies in the Safety Zones, I speak to you today because the specter of annihilation is upon us. The government and its Security Forces have made an assault on our freedom, annexing our land to turn it into factory monoculture farms to feed the ever growing appetite of its pacified population. Many lives were taken in the name of integration. They believe that they can kill or convert us all. The number of people being held in the so called social re-education camps is at an all-time high. We cannot allow these atrocities to continue."

I watch Turner lean in and whisper something in Chessed's ear before kissing her on the cheek and pushing his way back through the crowd. As he passes me, he gives me a dark look and ascends the stairs, shutting the metal door behind him without a sound.

"For too long this government has sought to control every aspect of our lives. For too long it has extracted our souls in exchange for security. You feel it in the air grown stale and thick with pollution. You hear it in the electric whir of engines they are trying so hard to silence because they know as long as you can hear it their illusion is not complete. Where once God made the clouds and brought the life-giving rain, we now pump heavy metals into the atmosphere to force their emergence ourselves.

"There was a magic once, in this life. A sense that there was something worth living for beyond the material. The rebel territories are the last stronghold of that hope. I am calling on you today to ask for your help."

Seeing my chance, I weave through the rows of onlookers and come up beside Chessed. She gives me a warm smile, a greeting in her eyes, but I pull her by the arm, gesturing with my head my desire to talk with her somewhere in private. Confused, she follows.

The Tok Rebellion

I lead her to a little storage room on the side of the hall. It used to hold barrels of wine back in the day, but Tok's team has converted it to an IT room where mismatched hardware blinks amid a maze of cables.

"What is it, Cassian?" she asks in a hushed voice. "What do you want?"

Outside we can still hear Tok's voice resonating in the stone chamber: "For those listening in the rebel territories, the time to strike back is now. The commanders of your militias have been alerted. We need every able-bodied person on the offensive. The future of our very existence is at stake."

"I... I don't know where we'll end up after this. I'm going to fight."

"Cassian..."

"I wanted to give you this. To remember me by." From my pocket I pull out the little pig figurine I had carved back on the farm.

"Don't talk like this."

"Please take it. I will never forget the time on your farm and what you showed me." She knows I cannot say I love her. She can see it in my eyes.

"And for those of you in the Safety Zones, those of you listening right now on the very Nets that imprison you, the fact that you have not yet turned off this message means that there is some part of you that is awake to the crimes of your corporations, of your President Zuck. You have been led to believe that your comfort is the ultimate goal, that there is nothing more in this life than that perfect stimulus that moment by moment recedes before you. Somewhere deep down inside you, you know that this will never satisfy. In fact, surrounded as you are by every pleasure imaginable, you have never felt more empty. This is the lie of your system, that one more thing will fix that ever-widening gulf in your heart.

"Today you are faced with a choice. You can spend the rest of your life groveling at the altar of pleasure and profit, or you can join me in a revolution that will shake this system down to the very foundations on which it stands."

There is no screaming because it comes exploding through the ceiling of the vault faster than the speed of sound, obliterating everything instantaneously. Chessed and I are thrown backward against the wall of the little storage room with the force of the blast. The ringing in my ears is so loud that I can hear nothing else. Coughing dust, I pull an old computer tower off Chessed. She is alive.

I help her up and we go stumbling out into the wreckage of the war room. Rubble is everywhere. Sunlight comes streaming down through the jagged hole that has been blown in the ceiling. From the world above there is the sound of gunfire.

The Tok Rebellion

"No, no, no, no..." Chessed says, rushing to the spot where Amy stood, pulling blocks of stone off the bodies there. "Amy, no," she pleads. But it is too late.

I hear a wheezing from the far side of the room. Someone is still alive.

It's Tok. His body is shredded beyond comprehension. I kneel beside him and prop his head up in my hand.

"In my pocket... inside pocket..." He spits up a stream of blood, splattering my face with his warm death. The words, "Last chance," are all he is able to utter before the light fades from his eyes.

I reach inside his jacket pocket and pull out a folded scrap of paper.

"Hey, there's still people alive down there," I hear a voice say from above, in the wreckage of the Exchange.

He is a Security Force soldier. He lets open fire a hail of bullets into the abyss below. I press myself up against the wall, out of the soldier's sight by only a few inches, and push the scrap of paper into my own pocket. I edge along the wall as bullets sink themselves into the rubble marked by violent puffs of dust.

"Chessed, we have to go, now."

"Amy... Jack... they're all dead."

"There's no time, Chessed. They're coming for us."

I help her up and we rush up the stairs into the passage. Flanking the door are the bodies of the two guards who had been stationed there. Their throats are cut and they lie in puddles of their own blood.

A few yards away Turner is crawling down the passage, banging his head with his fist. "Zafira, turn off. Zafira, I can't see anything. Turn off!"

"Turner!" Chessed yells and rushes to his side. "What's wrong?"

"Oh, Chessed, I didn't expect... Can you help me? Something's gone wrong with my eyes."

"What were you saying? Who's Zafira?"

"Zafira is the primary bot of the NeuralNet framework," I say, coming up beside them.

"I don't understand," Chessed says.

"He's lying!" Turner spits. "Stupid fucking liberal scum. You should be dead! Chessed, darling, help me. I can't see a thing. I think I've gone blind."

"He's not blind," I say. "His Net is glitching out from the explosion. He's a spy, Chessed. Feel behind his left ear. It will be higher up, behind his hairline, where we wouldn't notice it."

Chessed runs her finger through Turner's hair and he smacks her hand away.

"Oh my God, you have one. You have a Net." Face pale, she stands still, letting the new reality of the situation fall into place. Her fingers float up to her quivering lip. "Turner, I don't understand. This just doesn't make any sense." There's still a hint of something sweet in her voice, anger cracking through.

The Tok Rebellion

"Chessed, he's the one who called in this strike," I say. "He sent them our location."

"You left," she says in disbelief. "You left me in that room to die."

"Darling, I would never, I—it wasn't me," Turner says, scrambling blindly backwards until he's pressed up against the wall.

She grabs the automatic rifle from one of the dead guards and fires a shot into the ground by his feet. "How much did they pay you, huh? What was the price on his head?" she screams, pressing the barrel of the gun into Turner's cheek. "What was the price on his head?"

"Darling, please don't. They got to me early on. Gambling debts. After this I was going to be clear. I promise. I was going to buy us a nice big farm."

"And what about my farm? Was it you who told them where it was? Where to attack? Is my father dead because of you?"

"No... No... I—"

She fires the gun above his head sending little bits of rock tumbling down his face.

"You were probably surprised to see me alive after that. Figured I would have been killed in the ambush, didn't you?"

At the end of the hall, the sound of a skirmish erupts, gun flashes lighting up the adjoining passage.

191

"We have to go, Chessed," I say, taking the rifle and a handgun from the other guard.

"Please don't kill me," Turner slobbers, eyes searching upward for her face through the incoherent jumble of ads and error screens that cloud his vision.

Chessed lets out a primal yowl. The struggle in the next passage is getting closer.

"If you're going to kill him, you have to do it now."

She looks upon her betrayer with a mixture of pity and contempt. Her finger hovers over the trigger. "How could you?" is all she says and coming from her mouth it is more devastating than any bullet. She removes the gun from his face and starts off down the passage with me following close behind her.

"Thank you, thank you," he calls up, beseeching the woman who is no longer there. "Thank you," he calls, his voice receding as we pass around a corner just as another bomb penetrates the tunnel, blowing the passage behind us to senseless unremembering bits.

61

The tunnels lead us down a labyrinth of passages until we emerge in the cellar of a house where the sound of fighting is distant. It's a safe house, of sorts. As safe as a house can be in a war with bunker-busting smart bombs. It was probably set up as an escape for Tok should things go wrong.

Things had gone horribly wrong.

We take food. We take ammunition. Outside is an old Land Cruiser, covered by a tarp and fallen pine needles. Chessed finds the keys in a drawer in the kitchen. The tank is full.

We load everything we can into the back. Blankets, a 6-gallon water jug, an extra car battery. I find three red gasoline canisters behind the house and strap them to the roof rack. There are camping supplies: a tent, sleeping bags, and bedrolls. We load it all.

Chessed hops behind the wheel and I take the passenger seat. She knows that I can't drive stick. We take a dirt road that follows the contour of the Yuba ravine. She turns down a rutted side road and drives us, bouncing over rocks, to a promontory.

She cuts the engine and we get out and look. In the distance, beyond the forest, there are explosions, huge plumes of smoke, the remains of Nevada City being bombed out of existence.

And further out, all along the foothills, are more plumes and clouds of black where the last rebel cities are being snuffed out forever.

ANGELS

62

It's just me and Chessed now. We are heading over the mountains to the desert. To the spot on the map that Tok said was our last chance. It took a while to correspond Tok's fragment with the outdated map of U.S. highways we found in the Land Cruiser, but when we located it using the sparse names of hills and drainages, we set off to find it. There was nothing else to do.

The 80 would be patrolled so we stick to dirt roads, some so rough I'm sure the Land Cruiser will pop a tire. We don't talk much. There is not much to say.

In the afternoon we stop to eat something. Beneath a sugar pine we spoon beans into our mouths straight from the can, staring blankly at the insects and dust motes that float, sunlit and unconcerned with the problems of our world.

When we go to pack up, I notice something in the sky. "Look." It's a white oval, so high up that I can hardly make out its shape. "What is that?"

"What?"

"See, right there, almost straight up above us."

"Oh yeah. That is odd."

"It's not moving. It could be a spy balloon or something. Maybe they're watching us."

"If they were watching us, don't you think they would have bombed us already?"

"Yeah, I guess so. But what the heck could it be?"

"I don't know, Cassian."

63

"Even with the extra gas canisters, we're going to need to refuel somewhere," I say, looking at the map. "There's this little town. It's close to the 80, but they might have a working gas station."

"Are there any other options?" Chessed asks, looking weary behind the wheel.

"We could try to find a cabin. There's bound to be a car somewhere we can siphon the fuel out of. There's a lake. Altair Lake. We can look there."

"Okay."

I navigate us down a network of old logging roads until we reach the edge of a blue mountain lake. I get out and splash the cool water on my war-ravaged face, gray residue dripping off me and spoiling the crystal clear surface.

"Look, over there, on the opposite shore. There's a cabin, Cassian."

We take the Cruiser down the road that follows the edge of the lake past multiple "No Trespassing" signs, when, around a blind curve, Chessed slams on the brakes to avoid hitting an old woman in a nightgown.

The woman, white hair astray at messy angles, is yelling and gesticulating at us through the clouds of dirt kicked up by the tires.

"Why the fuck were you driving so fast? Can't you read the signs?"

Chessed rolls down her window. "We're sorry, miss. Truly. We didn't think anyone would be out here."

"Well, I suppose that's all right. Say, you're a cute one aren't you? And your husband's not so bad on the eyes either."

"Oh, he's not my..."

"What are you two doing out here anyway? Usually don't get strangers up at the lake since the summer camp closed down."

"Well, ma'am, we were looking for gas."

"You know they got a station in Sierraville. Unless you're running on empty that is. Then I could probably help you out. I think I got some old canisters around my place somewhere."

The Tok Rebellion

"Thank you ma'am. We didn't think Sierraville was safe with the war going on and all."

"War? Oh yes. Hank mentioned something about that the last time he visited. Fighting and all that. Horrible business."

"It's gotten worse, ma'am. We think the whole State of Jefferson has been taken."

"Oh dear."

"Would you like a ride back to your house?"

"I suppose that would be nice."

64

Her cabin is spacious, modern, built before the Reset with a loft and tall double-paned windows overlooking the lake. "Would you like any tea?" the old woman asks. She takes tiny steps, the only kind that her old frame will allow, setting a kettle on her wood-burning stove before we even answer.

"Yes," I say. "That would be lovely."

"We were in Nevada City this morning," Chessed says. "They bombed it. There's nothing left."

"Seems like someone's always fighting someone, doesn't it?" Sophia replies, hobbling over to the couch opposite us and easing herself into a seated position.

The Tok Rebellion

"This is bad, ma'am," Chessed continues.

"Please, call me Sophia."

"Sophia, their aim is to integrate everyone. They'll put you in a camp. They'll make you get a Net."

"No one much came up here back when this was the United States. No one much came up here when it was the State of Jefferson. Just my Hank. Don't suppose it will be much different now."

"Is Hank your husband?" I ask.

"He's my son. He brings me food and supplies every couple weeks. He's a good son. My only one. I love him dearly."

Chessed and I exchange concerned looks. "Well, we'd be happy to trade you for gas if you need anything, Sophia. We've got tons of canned food and some tools in our car," She suggests.

"I've got so many cans of beans stocked away I'll probably be dead before I finish them all. Oh, there's the water." She gets up at the whistling of the kettle and ambles over to the stove. "I learned a tea ceremony back when I used to travel. Would you like me to show it to you?"

"I don't know if..." Chessed begins.

"We would love that," I say. "Thank you."

"I'm not sure if I remember all the steps correctly. It's been a long time since I performed it for anyone."

"I'm sure whatever you remember will be great."

Sophia fishes in her cupboard and brings back three ceramic cups, handleless, and sets them on the table. From a drawer she produces a long olive-toned cloth and lays it across the table then sets the cups out in a row on top of it. "To catch any spills," she says, winking.

On the table is an unglazed teapot with a handle on the side, the lid is cracked and held together with some glue. There is also a wide bowl, a piece of bamboo cut in half lengthwise so as to create a kind of shoot, an incense holder and a slender stick of incense.

"We also need some nature. Cassian, would you be a dear and fetch some leaves from my maple tree out front?"

When I return, Sophia has a disc of something the size of a small frisbee wrapped in ornamental paper.

"I've been saving this tea cake for years. It's from the '90s. Same year I met my husband."

She takes the maple leaves from me and places them with aesthetic precision on the corners of the cloth. Then, with her delicate and trembling hands, she unwraps the circular cake of pressed black tea leaves. Using a butter knife, she breaks into it, chipping off crumbling pieces of the fermented mass. "That should be enough for us, don't you think?" she says, placing the freed leaves in the little bamboo shoot. "Now it's traditional to do three cups in silence."

The Tok Rebellion

We nod in agreement. She pours steaming water directly from the kettle into the teapot then into the cups. These she drains into the bowl. This step baffles me before I realize it is to warm the items before use.

Next, she dumps the tea from the bamboo into the pot and rinses the aromatic leaves with more hot water before draining the first steeping into the wide bowl as well, for an ancestor perhaps. At last, the pot is filled to the brim and, after saying a silent prayer over the vessel, she fills our cups.

The tea is dark, rich, and smells of a forest floor, damp with the regeneration of decay. It sits in little amber pools in the cups like portals to another world. When we finish a round, Sophia pours more, spinning the liquid in a counterclockwise motion using the angle of the spout.

Something about this tea makes me feel like the trees are speaking to me from across time, transferring some wisdom to me that can only be known by roots and wood and seasons. We sit, covered in the residue of war, sipping from fragile china a drink of meditation.

When we finish the third pouring and set our cups back in a row, she bows and we bow back.

"Thank you," I say.

"That was beautiful," Chessed says. Tears are running down her face. "Can I give you a hug?"

"Of course," Sophia says and Chessed embraces her, holding her like an old friend.

"I'm sorry," she says, wiping away her tears. "We've had a hard day."

"No need to apologize, dear. The tea is a heart opener. That's why I like it."

Chessed takes her seat again next to me and places her hand on my knee, looking at me with a knowing gratitude. We have both been through so much.

"Now, if you don't object, I'll give you a tarot reading."

"Tarot?" I say.

"Why yes. Tea and tarot go together, well, like tea and tarot."

She produces from a drawer in a side table a deck of cards wrapped in a purple silk scarf. Moving the tea paraphernalia to the side, she lays out the scarf and the cards contained within.

"Shuffle the deck," she instructs. "I'll do a reading for the both of you."

I sift through the cards, rearranging their order, then tapping them back into a neat stack. Chessed does the same.

"First, your past," Sophia says, taking the deck and flipping over the top card. "Ahh, the Five of Cups." She places the card on the left side of the scarf. On it there is a figure in a long black cloak, head bowed in sorrow and surrounded by golden chalices, some knocked over, some still standing.

The Tok Rebellion

"This is a card of deep sadness. You have lost a lot. The person on the card is distraught that their cups have been spilled. Wine pools on the ground like blood. But look, one of the cups held a green liquid. It was poison. Perhaps it's not so bad that this cup was lost.

"But this card is not all sad. Look on his right side. He still has two cups standing. There are still two left that can cross the river and reach the destination beyond. Does this make any sense?"

"Weirdly, yes," I say.

"Weird indeed," she replies. "The cards never lie." She cuts the deck in half. "Now for the present." She flips over another card and places it in the center of the scarf. There is an old man on a throne. Through an archway you see people talking, unconcerned with the king.

"The Ten of Pentacles. This card depicts a man near the end of his life who has amassed a great fortune and given his children a life of luxury. But the children do not realize what they have. They are ignorant of the sacrifices of their father. The card is reversed. It may take you a while to realize what it means."

She takes a deep breath, looking first at Chessed, then at me. "Now for your future." She flips a final card. On it, an angel trumpets, and corpses rise from the grave. "Judgement."

Our fortune teller settles back into the plush leather couch, sunlight glinting off the lake behind her like so many coins. Her eyes are bright, lucid. "This was my husband's card. Houston. It always came up whenever I did a reading for him. He always took it to mean that he judged himself for what he did. That's not the meaning of the card though. Ten years into our marriage, when we were still raising Hank, he came to me wanting a divorce. He was having an affair. He said I didn't deserve him. I told him that was not up to him to decide. If we were going to end everything we built together, we both had to make that choice. And I chose to stay with him."

"You should have left him," Chessed says.

"That's what my friends said too. They said I was weak. Some didn't talk to me for years. But life isn't about doing what's easy. Sometimes you choose the hard road knowing full well it will not make you happy. I chose to stay with Houston because the depth of our relationship was more important to me than revenge, than freedom, than my own happiness. It seems crazy, I know. But God put me here in his shoes to have a hard meaningful life. You could say I'm a glutton for punishment, but I learned more about myself from staying with that man than I ever could have by leaving him. Marriage is like a crucible. You are forged pure by the excruciating torment."

"You had a chance to start over and you chose to stay the path," I say.

The Tok Rebellion

"Exactly. Ending something only creates new devils. I stayed and new, beautiful, horrible emotions emerged from me, the likes of which I did not think were possible. Perhaps we weren't sent here to seek the good. After all, God has spent an eternity in love and light. Maybe the good is boring to him. Maybe through us, he can at last learn to suffer."

65

Sophia gives us enough gas to fill our tank and a few of our canisters. We thank her for her hospitality. She asks if she can ride with us to the end of her driveway. She likes to wait there for her son, Hank, she says.

We leave her in our rearview mirror, still in her nightgown, standing on the shore of her lake. "I don't know if Hank's going to come back," Chessed says. "It looked like just about every rebel city had been bombed."

"We don't know that for sure. And who knows, maybe he did die, but she seems like a woman who could handle that truth."

The Tok Rebellion

We drive on through high mountain meadows where the trees are replaced by seas of flowing yellow grass. At some point, we must have crossed the divide because the streams flow east now and there is a slow descent to the land and behind us the sun that sets is red with smoke.

We find an old abandoned forest service campground and take up a spot with a metal fire ring and bear box. Site number 9. Our dinner is jerky and tortillas and more beans, heated this time over a modest campfire. The spigot two sites over on the trail to the vault toilets works, fed no doubt by some spring further up the hill.

I set up the tent while Chessed lays on the picnic table looking up at the stars. "That thing is still up there," she says.

I crane my neck and, indeed, straight overhead is the same oval shaped object, now shining like a bright planet in the night sky.

"The government must be really curious what we're up to."

"I don't think it's the government," she says.

"What, you mean, like, aliens?"

"I don't know. But it feels benevolent. Like a bird on a branch, just watching us."

"They have these things called geostationary satellites. It could be one of those."

"It seems too close to be a satellite."

I take the tent. Chessed sleeps in the back of the Land Cruiser and as I fall asleep the bright shining light of the visitor does not waver, glowing there in the darkness like some unknowable harbinger of things yet to come.

66

In the morning there are three of them, following us in a triangular formation at the zenith of the sky. It feels like we are fulfilling some prophecy from a forgotten time. The back dirt roads take us ever lower through pine then juniper then rock canyons, depositing us at last onto the flat barren basins of Nevada.

Tok's map takes us into remote land punctuated only by bitter mountains, singular islands surrounded by expanses of mudcracks and grass. By noon there are five of them, just distinguishable next to the glaring explosion of the sun.

Nate Lemcke

The A/C is intermittent, producing irregular spurts of cold between long intervals of hot air. The way is long and there is nothing but static on every frequency accessible by the car radio.

We make camp on a seemingly infinite piedmont flowing off the foot of a mountain. Chessed gathers wild sage and bundles it together with bits of string. In the firelight, she burns the tip of the smudge stick and blows life into its glowing embers sending fragrant desert smoke cascading over my body as she moves the bundle in little circles around me like a magic wand with the power to heal the past.

"Now do me," she says.

She stands with arms outstretched at her sides, head tilted back, eyes closed in veneration. I blow on the smoldering sage until it glows bright orange, bits of burning stem and leaf breaking off and racing into the night. Starting from her head, I work down, caressing her with the smoke, evoking some lost sense of ritual. I trace her whole body with the glowing wand until at last I blow the smoke onto her feet, smudging away any traces of the evil that had been cast upon us.

That night we sleep under the stars—no tent, no truck—and, beneath the eyes of the watchers, for that is what we now call them, Chessed lays her head on my shoulder and wonders aloud how long is an age and what calamity marks its end.

67

The morning greets us with sunbeams arcing across the sky. We pack up our things and start off on the final segment of our journey to the spot Tok marked with an X and the letters "HAEMP." The dirt track road takes us up a mountain range where yuccas stand ten feet tall and their pale blossoms quiver in the breeze at the top of their stalks. Overhead, the watchers trail us, silent and ethereal, making no move save for those minute calculations that keep them anchored at our zenith.

We drive through a pygmy forest of juniper and pine where jackrabbits the size of small dogs bound away from the sound of the approaching SUV and ravens croak guttural intonations of doom from the branches of smitten trees. The road takes us past a vista overlooking a long saline valley. Somewhere on the valley floor there is a muted compound of gray metal structures.

We descend along a gutted wash where primordial rock layers are tilted and metamorphosed with winding bands of iron that mimic the very watercourse they now confine. Chessed grinds the ancient gearbox, putting the vehicle into low-4 over sections of road that have all but been reclaimed by nature.

Now out in the valley, the gentle toe of the mountain takes us down a washboard road so ribbed with undulations that the successive harmonizing bumps shake the entirety of the Land Cruiser, sending us bouncing in our seats like ragdolls. At one point the road becomes so sandy we have to get out and pave two tracks with scrub branches so that the tires have something to grip.

We pass along the shore of a primeval lake, long since evaporated into a white crystalline expanse. A misshapen windmill stands inexplicable on the shoreline, its two remaining vanes hanging defeated in the desolation of the valley.

The road ends at the fenced entrance to the compound and we pull up, unspeaking, to the gate.

The Tok Rebellion

Chessed gets out and laces her fingers through the chain link and I join her by her side.

"It's some sort of military base," I say. "Abandoned during the Reset by the looks of it." The guardhouse is empty. The door hangs loose on its hinges and papers flutter on the floor there.

"Why do you think Tok was so interested in this place?"

"I don't know. I guess we should look around."

"How do you plan on getting over the fence?"

It's at least twelve feet high and lined with razor wire.

"Hmm," I say, pulling experimentally on the locked gate. It's futile. "We could drape our blankets over the razor wire and climb over that way."

"Before we resort to that, let me see if there's anything in the truck that could cut through the fence."

As Chessed is rummaging around in the back of the Cruiser I hear a strange melodic humming. "Chessed... Chessed, look."

Above us, one of the watchers has broken rank with the others and descends with no visible propulsion system until it is poised floating over the guard house, like an obloid mirror reflecting everything around it in gleaming surreal proportions.

Chessed holds my hand, our hair fluttering in the presence of the phenomena.

Suddenly, the lights in the guard house come flickering to life and the gate jolts, rolling backward along its course until it recedes with a clank into a fully open position.

"I think it wants us to go inside," I say, in disbelief.

We pass through the gate. Once we are inside, the silvery ship floats over and lands in the dirt yard with a crunch of gravel. The humming stops and through some imperceptible hatch on the top of the saucer, a being emerges. It raises its hand towards us, three elongated fingers, and at once my sight is overcome with a vision.

I see a spreading metropolis, lights and smoke and causeways, extending mold-like and dendritic to the far reaches of the earth. I see animals fleeing, plants dying. I see rockets taking off from this planet like vectors containing a dangerous disease and injecting themselves on new planets to spread their cancer further. An apocalypse of technology and mechanization. "THIS FUTURE DOES NOT HAVE TO BE." The words are spoken directly into my brain as if I were still connected to a Net.

Then there is a new vision. A single rocket launching and a blinding flash of light, high in the atmosphere over the coast. As the flash fades, the lights below in the city start to go out, block by block, until the whole night side of the earth is shrouded in a quiet darkness.

The Tok Rebellion

Dawn peaks over the horizon, lighting a new day as people step out of their cars, dazed, into a world now made simple. I see bowhunters and people grinding corn and vines of ivy creeping over the skyscrapers until the world is once again an Eden.

The vision stops and when I can see my surroundings again, the being is gone but the ship remains. I look over at Chessed and I can tell from the wonder in her eyes that she has seen the same vision as me.

The ship once again emits its otherworldly hum and lifts off, gliding over us until it comes hovering above one of the buildings on the base. We follow.

The floodlights surrounding the building fluctuate in intensity as the ship induces a current in their worn-out circuitry. The keypad on an unmarked door lights up and the deadbolt retracts with a dull clunk. I turn the handle and the door swings open into a flickering fluorescent interior. We walk in together, still entranced with the power of the vision.

There is a harsh buzzing sound and all of the doors unlock simultaneously, swinging open to reveal cluttered bureaucratic offices, long since empty of their occupants.

An elevator at the end of the hall dings and opens. As erratic as the alien power supply seems to be, I suggest we take the emergency stairwell. We descend perhaps fifteen flights before the staircase bottoms out at a single door. I search Chessed's face for answers I know she cannot have. She merely nods. I push the door open.

Inside is a control room with a large screen. The air is stale, like a putrid scent once hung here before it too perished. There are two desks and behind each of them sits a withered corpse, now just dried skin and bones, dressed in military uniforms.

"I guess no one bothered to let them know they were relieved of duty," I say.

Chessed runs her hand along the terminal and the monitor springs to life displaying a low-resolution map of the world. There are crosshairs centered on Moscow and a single blinking cursor in a command line where one could enter new coordinates.

"HAEMP," I say, reciting Tok's inscription on the map. "High Altitude Electromagnetic Pulse. This is a missile silo, Chessed."

"Like a nuclear missile?"

"Yes, but not the kind that blows up on the ground. They're designed to detonate high in the atmosphere."

"What would be the point of that?"

"It emits an electromagnetic pulse that propagates through the atmosphere and disables any electronic device in the blast radius."

"You mean like the vision."

"Yes. It would shut off everyone's Net. But more importantly, if we detonated it over San Francisco it

The Tok Rebellion

would destroy the infrastructure at MetaLabs that everything runs on. Everything is so integrated that it would cause a domino effect shutting off the power grid and the global financial system."

"How do you know all this?"

"There were days I would daydream about it happening. I always thought it would come from Russia though."

Using the guides on the edge of the map for reference, I type in the approximate coordinates of San Francisco, and the crosshairs reappear over California.

Chessed goes up to the screen and fingers, beneath it, a small metallic keyhole. There is an identical one on the opposite side of the terminal. At 90° to the position of the slot, the word "Armed" is printed in efficient, utilitarian lettering. "We would need the keys," she says.

I search the corpse of the officer nearest to me and find around his neck a lanyard with a single key.

"It's set up so no one person could launch the missile," she says.

I retrieve the other lanyard and give it to her. "Cassian, if we do this, even if the bomb itself doesn't kill anyone, people will still die when everything shuts down. Just like my mom died. In the chaos."

"My parents live in San Francisco. My old friends. I don't know how many of them would survive without their Nets."

"But think of everyone they killed. Think of the farm, of my dad. Of Amy and Jack and everyone else in Nevada City."

"How is this our choice? This shouldn't be a choice anyone should have to face."

"The watchers, they wanted us to do this. That's why they followed us here."

"If they wanted it so much, why didn't they just do it themselves?"

"It's the fate of our planet. Our species. I think they wanted us to decide."

Thank you, Sara Ulrika Holopainen,
for your unflagging insight. Your contributions to this work
were indispensable.

And thank you, Elizabeth Nichin, for seeing what I couldn't.